GOLDEN SHOWERS

GOLDEN SHOWERS

Written By Shirley Jordan

authorHOUSE®

AuthorHouse™
1663 Liberty Drive
Bloomington, IN 47403
www.authorhouse.com
Phone: 1 (800) 839-8640

Published by AuthorHouse 07/09/2015

ISBN: 978-1-5049-2214-2 (sc)
ISBN: 978-1-5049-2213-5 (e)

The Golden Shower

I was twenty two years old and a senior in college, when I met a handsome soldier man, fresh from the military. It had to be love at first sight, because we were inseparable. We did everything together. My soldier friend didn't seem to have a mean streak in his body. He was soft spoken, always smiling and he loved kissing, hugging and holding hands. My sister loved the way he cherished me. She thought he brought out the best in me. But actually, I brought out the best in him. He was a loner. He didn't have any friends, so we shared my same friends. He thought it was more appropriate to be around other couples to motivate each other to stay together. He thought having a friend that was single would complicate things. Because a single person didn't have the same respect for their significant other. He said a single person was quick to give up on a friendship because they didn't understand the strategy of being a couple. He felt as if a single person would tell a person that's in a relationship not to take whatever the problem would be. Instead of helping their friends see the problem as a mild stepping stone.

I understood what he was saying, because I had been in a situation where I went to my single friend for an opinion and she didn't try to fix the situation. She would rather let that person go and start over with someone else. But I was single too. And at that time, I didn't want to take the unnecessary drama either. I was one of the ones that were ready to get out and move on. I thought I had better things to do with my life, than to deal with a man that wasn't on my level. I don't think a single person would try to break up a relationship, if they knew the couple was in love and they thought the relationship was worth saving.

My soldier friend loved taking trips. I was just a few credits from graduating College, when he booked to a trip to Africa for us. We would take cruises, travel to different countries and talk about his days in the service. He would tell me how strict his sergeant would be to the solders. He said the sergeant was extremely mean to him, because he would rather do things his way, instead of following the correct procedures of the military, but it is known. When you are in the military, it's their way or no way.

He even talked about how bad he wanted out of the military, but the military wouldn't let him go, without it being a dishonorable discharge. Getting a dishonorable discharge was not accepted in his family's household. He told me, his father was as mean and strict as the sergeant in the military, if not meaner.

He had a lot of horrifying stories to tell and I would sit and listen to them all.

He was a good man, with a lot of mysteries. I could feel there was something, he wasn't telling me, but I left well enough alone. I said to myself. He will tell me when he's ready. I thought, maybe it was too soon into the relationship for him to tell me everything about what had happened to him.

Some of his stories were straight out of a horror movie. I sometimes wondered how he managed to live as long as he did. He had a strange feeling about people leaving his life. I thought it was because of something that happened to him in the military. So I would hold him close to me and tell him how safe he was with me.

It was hard for him to really trust anyone. He said that every time he would put his heart into someone, they would always find away to let him down. So I made him a promise that he could trust me and I would never leave him.

We never married, but we moved into a one bedroom townhome, with the master bedroom and study upstairs with the kitchen and a half bathroom downstairs. Shortly after moving in together we began to have little arguments about the living arrangements in the home. This opened up a hold new door for me. I began to see the military side of him and it was pretty scary. I found out later that those words about me never leaving him were the wrong words to say to a military man. He made me live up to those words for the rest of our relationship. I found out the hard way that you never leave a soldier behind.

In the beginning, we seemed to agree on lots of things. We were so compatible. But as the relationship lasted, the more he began to change. Nothing I said or did seemed to be right. He had become very controlling. I felt like I was in the military, and he was the mean sergeant drilling my every life skills. I would tell myself, he was just acting strange, because of him being in the military for too long, and then I would do some of the things the way he wanted them done.

We had our first real argument after living together for two years. I had dropped out of college to spend more time with him, with the intentions of going back. After two years of having fun, I was ready to go back to school.

I could have done the credits I had left for getting my degree online. But I liked on hands schooling. I liked being around other people, it made feel like I was actually in school, with friends, trying to accomplish something. But as I was preparing myself to go back to school, I found out I was pregnant. I had less than a year to complete my degree. I had to postpone it again because of being pregnant.

Well as it turned out, he wasn't ready for a child. He wanted me to go back to school to get my degree like I had planned. He thought a baby would only put off the things I had planned to do with my life. I didn't believe in abortions, and I didn't want to do both, being pregnant and going to school together. I wanted to enjoy being pregnant. So I told him that I wanted to wait another year after the baby was born. This sent him into a horrific rage. I had never seen this side of him before. He grabbed me by the arm and threw me to the bed. Then he jumped on top of me tearing off my clothes. Just before he got to my panties, he stopped. He began to cry and begged me to forgive him for his actions. I never saw him act that way. I was puzzled and I just didn't understand what was going on in his head. So I forgave him.

The following month, I wasn't feeling well, so I didn't have dinner ready when he came home from work. We got into a huge argument because the kitchen had a few dishes in the sink and there was no dinner cooked. I was on my way down stairs to make dinner and he pushed me down the stairs, causing me to lose our unborn child. Now this could have been an accident because I was standing at the edge of the stairway, getting ready to take a step down. I wasn't completely sure if he pushed me on purpose. Knowing, I would fall from the top of the stairs and lose our baby. Even though he was upset, I couldn't bring myself to think that he would push me down those stairs on purpose. No one could be that evil.

He rushed to the hospital. He had a look on his face as he has just done something so horrible. So when the doctors asked what happened? I lied and said my baby daddy startled me, which caused me to fall down the stairs.

I wanted to believe in my heart, I wasn't with a man that would stoop as low as to pushing me down the stairs to get rid of my pregnancy.

This was the beginning of all my troubles. The look on his face was a look of release. He was so happy, I didn't tell the doctor what really happened. He said, he loved me so much for tell that lie, and then he held me so tight. I had to push him away, because he was hurting me.

That first lie turned in to many more. I found myself lying about black eyes, busted lips and broken bones. Each time his apologies were more and more sincere. Depending on the pain and my reactions, he would break down and cry. He would sit on the floor holding himself and yell how sorry he was for the pain he caused me. He would sometimes leave the house for a couple of days, and when he would come back home. He would be a totally different person. And again, I would blame the military and forgive him. It seemed crazy, but for some reason I felt sorry for him.

During the first three years I lived with him, I never tried to leave him. No matter how bad the situations would be, I would stay. I felt, he needed me. I continued to put his actions on the military. This way, it may it easier for me to deal with his mood swings.

My family and friends were so in love with this man. I thought if I was to leave him, they would be mad at me. If I was to say anything negative about him, they wouldn't believe it, because he had such a sweet personality when he was around them. He would open doors, pull out chairs and compliment all the women in sight. He was the perfect gentleman.

All of my friends would tell me how lucky I was to have such a good man. My sister would tell me, she was proud of me too. She thought my man was so good to me. She couldn't wait for me to get married. She wanted to be the one to do all of the wedding plans. I never told anyone about the things I was going through with my man. I just supported him, because of the look on his face, when he hears all of the good things other women had to say about him.

I knew I had a good man, because he was a man that took good care of the responsibilities for the house. He made sure that I was well taken care of. He wanted me to have the better of the two cars we had. Even though he knew how to fix cars, he didn't want me stranded somewhere due to a car problem. He didn't mind cleaning, he loved to cook and he does gardening work around the house on his free time.

He was a very strict man. I would never know what to expect at times. He would have different mood swings when he would come home from where ever he would be. He couldn't stand for a woman to question his whereabouts or inputs. There have been times when I asked where he's been and it would start an argument. So I learned to wait until he started a conversation. This way I could ease a question in without him knowing. I hated arguing. But somehow, I could always make him upset with something that I would say.

He would put on such a good act around my family. Bringing me flowers and expensive gifts while kissing my forehead and massaging my neck. But if only my sister knew that he was doing all of these nice things for me, because of what he had done to me the night before. They couldn't see that it was all done out of guilt, for the pain that he had caused me. Sometimes I wondered if he was only coming around with gifts to see if I had told anyone about the horrible times we were having. He wanted to keep what ever happened in our home, to stay in our home. He said that it was no one's business to know what went on in our home and he wanted to keep it that way. I didn't have any intentions of telling anyone, because I didn't want anyone to tell me I was wrong for staying with him. If there was any reason for leaving a man, it would be the reason for abuse. Rather it was mental or physical.

I knew that he was a good man, but there was something going on in his head that I just couldn't figure out. I felt that it was something that happened while he served in the military, but I didn't know what. Whenever I tried talking about the military, he would change the subject. He would sometimes come to me crying for no apparent reason. He would be on his knees begging me not to leave him. I told him that I had made him a promise and I would never break that promise.

Things really began to get rough for me as time went on. One day I had the house cleaned and dinner ready, but I didn't make the bed because I was lying in bed talking on the phone with my best friend from college. When he got home, he asked me if I would fix him a plate of food. I didn't respond to him quick enough. So he came upstairs and snatched the phone away from me. He asked if I heard him. And I replied, "Yes." He then through the phone and grabbed me by the neck. My best friend was still on the phone. She was listening to everything that was going on. When he realized he didn't hang up the phone, he went to pick it up and my friend was still it. He told her that I would have to call her back. He said that I had to use the restroom and afterwards we were going to have dinner together. This was my chance to get away from him. So I ran into the bathroom and sat on the toilet to get my thoughts together. I'm not sure of what my friend heard, but my man was good at changing things to make you feel like everything is going find. So she told him to tell me she would call me later. After hanging up the phone he came to the bathroom door and began to bang on it. He asked me to come out, but I refused. He then started kicking the door. He kicked until he kicked the door open.

He snatched me off the toilet, threw me to the floor, pulled down his pants and began to urinate on me. As he was urinating, he said that I belonged to him and no one else. He said if I would try to leave him, he would always find me. He said if anyone was to get in the way of our relationship. He would kill them. After urinating on me, he said that he had marked his territory and no other dog could touch me. I felt so belittled. I had never heard of such a thing.

Was he calling me a female dog?

Telling me that he had marked his territory and no other dog could touch me. I was really afraid of him at this point. But I knew I had to stay calm. So I asked him if I could take a shower. He told me no. He said that I could shower, when he said I could shower and no before. Then he told me to wash my hands, go downstairs and fix him a plate of food. I didn't want to stir up anymore drama. So I went downstairs, smelling like urine and took his plate of food out of the microwave. When I brought him his food, he patted me on the head and said, "Good girl." I then knew the answer to my question. He was calling me a female dog.

After he finished his food, he wanted us to shower together. So I agreed. When we got into the shower, he was a perfect gentleman. He bathed me as if nothing had happen. After bathing me, he began kissing me on the neck while he cleaned himself. We made love and it was the most passionate love making that we had ever made. Then he bathed me again. This time, he wanted to make love from behind. He wanted to pretend to be dogs. I was afraid to say no. We had sex in the shower a second time. But this time he was extremely rough with me. I had so many thoughts going on in my head, because I was trying not to think of the pain he was putting me through. I really didn't know this person. I had just made passionate love with him, now the love making was totally demeaning.

I was thinking, should I call the police?

Should I leave him, when he was sound asleep?

Do I tell people what he had done to me?

Would anyone believe me, if I told them what had just happened to me?

I just didn't know what to do, or who to tell what I was going through.

After he told me he would hurt anyone that would try to help me leave him. I thought it was best for me to just stay with him to see if his behavior would change.

But what if his behavior didn't change?

Would I eventually be killed by this man?

I knew he loved me. There was no reasonable doubt about that. I loved him too, but I was afraid to leave. I promised him I would never leave him and I'm a woman of my word, and I always have been. So when I told him I would never leave him, I meant it. So I decided to stay.

I thought to myself that he had always been a good provider and he was always loyal to me. He showed me in many ways, how much he loved me and wanted to be with me. So I tried weighing all the good times with the bad times to see if it would give me a reason to leave him. But I came up with nothing. So I decided to stay. I looked deep down into this man's heart and I found nothing but love for me. That's when I knew I had just made the right choice. We were good together. We both had lots of things that we enjoyed doing together and I think that's why I loved him as much as I did. I just had to over look his mental problem or try to help him fix it.

The bad times had seemed to have gone away. It was about a year later and we had no bad incidents. Yes, we argued, but it never got to the point where I wanted to leave him. We took a trip to New Mexico, the Caribbean Islands and Miami Florida just to get away, so we could share each other's love without any interruptions from friends and family. At the time I thought it was a great idea. I loved traveling and so did he. But each time we made it back home from a trip. He would get upset with me. He didn't like me talking on the phone telling my friends and family how much fun we had. He thought I was taking up his time, by talking on the phone. He wanted me for himself. He didn't like sharing me with anyone. So he would book us on another trip.

It took my friend to get me to notice the strange behavior. She reminded me of what happened when we were on the phone and my boyfriend came home and wanted all of my attention. She told me that he didn't want to share me with anyone. She said he had become controlling and unpredictable. He just wanted me for himself and I wasn't the type of person that just wanted to stay stuck under a man and have no life of my own. I told my friend I understood how she felt, but when we go away on trips, we really enjoy ourselves. I told her not to worry about me. I said she had put too much into the last incident that she heard on the phone. I tried to convince her that everything was fine. But we were friends for too long and she knew something wasn't right by the sound of my voice.

Not knowing my boyfriend had come home from work early to surprise me with good news about his job promotion. He was listening to my conversation. This time he waited until I got off the phone and walked into the room. When I asked him why was he home so early. He grabbed my face and began to squeeze my cheeks very hard. I thought he was going to squeeze out some of my teeth as hard as he was squeezing my cheeks. I couldn't move my head and I couldn't pull his hands off my face. He had a really tight grip. When he finally let go, I kicked him in the stomach. I could see that I had just made a bad mistake. His eyes had gotten so big and his face had turned red. I knew I had just made the biggest mistake, since we had been together, by kicking him between his legs. He grabbed me by my hair and snatched me out of the bed. I tried to get away but he was just too strong. He pulled me into the bathroom and began to unzip his pants. I knew what was going to happen next. So while he was unzipping his pants. I tried to turn over onto my knees so I could run out of the bathroom. But I wasn't strong enough. I was able to turn over. But I couldn't pull his hands off my hair. He aimed at the back of my head and began to urinate. I was showered from the back of my head to the back of my thighs. This made me very angry, so I turned around and began to fight. My first hit was to his face. This made him even angrier, but I didn't care this time. I didn't think it was fair for him to urinate on me. I was not an animal and I refused to be treated like one. So I wanted to give him a taste of his own medicine. I ran to the restroom downstairs and used the cup on the counter to urinate. Then I ran back upstairs and threw the urine on him. Then I asked him how it felt to be treated like a dog. When he smelt, I threw urine on him. It only made matters worse. I saw him running towards me in a rage. So I tried to run downstairs, but I wasn't fast enough. He grabbed me by the hair and pulled me into the bedroom. He was trying to close the bedroom door, but my leg was in the way. Not knowing my leg was the reason the door wouldn't close. He tried slamming the door harder. I let out a loud scream and began to cry. He looked down and saw my leg caught between the door way. He tried to move it but I screamed louder. He began to cry, saying that he was sorry. He said he didn't know my leg was caught in the door. He asked if I could move my leg and I said, "No." He asked if he should call for help or should he take me to the emergency room himself. I didn't think my leg was broken, because the pain was bearable. We both smelled like urine, so I asked him to put me into the tub and wash me clean so I didn't smell like I urinated on myself when I got to the hospital.

We both smell awful. So he wanted to take a shower together. He asked if I could stand. I said, "No." So he took me a shower lying down in the tub and afterwards, he took himself a shower. After we both us were cleaned, he asked what was I going to tell the doctors, if they asked me what happened. I told him that I was going to tell them the truth. I said that I was going to tell them, we had an argument and he slammed the door on my leg, not knowing I was trying to stop him from closing the door. He then asked me if I thought he would go to jail for slamming the door on my leg. I felt the sadness in his heart and I knew it was an accident because he really didn't know my leg was in the door. So I told him not to worry. I knew how to handle the situation. The doctors took x-rays and I had a fractured bone, from where the door was shut on my leg. I was later released from the hospital with a hard cast on my leg. I had to stay off my leg for six weeks.

When I got home, I had my boyfriend to call my job and let them know I would have to stay home from work for a month and a half. It was hard for me, because I really liked my job. The people I worked with were friendly and we all got along as a team.

My boyfriend catered to my every need. He was a really good provider when I needed him to be. It was like being on a trip alone with him. Sometimes he would leave. But he always came home in a good mood, ready to take care of me. He was pretty streak about the doctors. So he refused to let me use my broken leg. I tried to look at it as a good thing. After all, the doctor did say I shouldn't use it for at least six weeks. But I knew I couldn't stay off of my let that long. So the times, he would leave me. I would stand up and move around the room looking for my cell phone. He wanted me to get complete rest and he said that means no talking on the phone. So he took my phone away from me.

I knew some of the people that worked at the hospital. And someone must have told my best friend about my accident. When my friend heard about the incident, she came by to visit. My boyfriend actually, opened the door and let her in to visit me and then he left us to be alone. She asked me if my boyfriend had something to do with my ankle being in a cast. I told her yes, but it really was an accident. She didn't believe me, so she said if I came up with anything else broken or bruised, she was going to make sure I got out of the abusive relationship. I knew my friend meant well. But I didn't want her to get involved in the crazy mess that I had gotten myself into. It wouldn't be fair for the both of us to get hurt. I didn't say much, and she knew, I was hiding something from her.

We had been best friends since the second grade and we always took good care of each other. We knew each other so well. We could tell when something wasn't right with one or the other. We always had the best interest for each other. She was an only child and I was the baby of four children.

I had been on my job every since I dropped out of college and I had never missed a day of work, without calling in. So when I broke my leg, my boyfriend had forgotten to call to let them know, I would be out of work for six weeks.

One of my co-workers came by to check on me and I wasn't able to answer the door. I wasn't sure if it was a trick that my boyfriend was playing, just to see if I would get out of bed to answer the door. But that day, I had taken some medicine that put me in such a dizzy position. I just decided to go to sleep. I really didn't hear anyone at the door. So when she went back to work the next day. She let it be known that she came over to my house and got no answer. This made everyone at work kind of nervous. So they made the decision to call the police if I didn't come in to work the next day. Well before they could call the police. I called and apologized for not calling the day before. I told them that I told my boyfriend to call and he forgot. The secretary told me that they were just about to call the police, if they hadn't heard anything from me that day. I again apologized and told the secretary that I had a broken leg and the doctors had me off work for six weeks. She notified the boss and he approved my leave of absence. This was the first time I had taken off due to an illness. All the other times I took off, were either vacation time or personal time off because of trips my boyfriend and I had taken. But I would always communicate with someone at work, just to let them know I was okay.

But, this time was different. I had accumulated a lot of friends at work, but it was for work and work only. I didn't want to have my incidents that were going on at my house, posted on the walls at work by gossip. Maybe that's why I didn't notice when one of my co-workers stopped by to check on me.

But, it was good to know that someone did care enough to come by and check up on me, because I didn't show up for work. I never told my boyfriend about a co-worker coming over. I wasn't sure if it would trigger another argument. So I decided to do a don't ask, don't tell situation. If he didn't ask, I didn't tell and it worked out just find.

The six weeks went by pretty fast. I was back to work in no time. My boss and I were pretty close work buddies. He knew about my boyfriend and I knew about his wife and two sons. He had me on a short term disability leave of absence. So I got paid for being off work. When I returned to work, my boss asked me out for lunch and I accepted the offer. We went to a new restaurant that had recently opened. It was a nice Chinese restaurant with a turning grill table and chefs would cook your food and entertain you while you ate. It was a very nice lunch. We enjoyed the entertainment while he caught me up with the work history, I missed for six weeks.

When we got back to work, the secretary had four notes for me. Each one was from my boyfriend. Since I wasn't at work to receive my messages, he decided to come up to my job and wait for me in the parking lot. When my boss and I drove up, my boyfriend was waiting and watching. My boss was such a gentleman. He always opened doors for his female passengers. So when my boyfriend saw my boss opening the door for me. He became very angry. He jumped out of his car. Ran over to my boss's car and began to talk extremely loud. My boss told me, that he would let me handle the situation, because we were at work and he didn't want to cause a scene at the job, while he was on duty. He then locked his car doors and walked away. My boyfriend on the other hand, wasn't finish with his conversation with my boss. So he decided to follow him back to the building and up to the work place. I tried to stop him, but he was out of control. So I told him if he was to keep up the confusing, my boss was going to call the police. For some reason, my boyfriend was afraid of the police. When I mentioned the police, he calmed down and left the building. I didn't know if he went home or not, but he left my work place.

Later on my boss called me into his office. He wanted to know if I was alright. I told him that my boyfriend's bark was worst than his bite. Then I told him by the time I get home, he would have calmed down and ready for step two, which was love making. I told my boss not to worry about what had just happened. Then I told him that I would take care of everything when I got home. I gave him a smile and left his office. Not knowing what I was going home to, I prepared myself for the worst. I knew it wouldn't be nice. So I tried to prepare myself for whatever was going to happen next. I thought I was going home to another huge argument. But my boyfriend had something totally different in mind.

I got home before him, which was strange. So I decided to cook him a special dinner. Wow! What a mistake that was. My boyfriend accused me of fixing him a special dinner, because I had done something wrong and now I was trying to fix it, by cooking. He said I couldn't fix it with a nice meal. He asked me why the special meal, what did I do so wrong, that I had to come home and fix a special meal. I told him that it was just his imagination. There was nothing wrong for me to fix. I began to smile and that was the wrong thing to do at that time. My boyfriend slapped my face. The slap was so hard, my entire body turned before I hit the floor. I knew something was going to happen, when I smiled at him. But I didn't think it would be a blow to my face. This was the first time my boyfriend had ever hit me in such a manner. I didn't know what to expect next. So I stayed on the floor with my arms covering my face. I thought if I was to lay there long enough, covering my face, he would leave the house. But he didn't. He decided to stand over me to see what damage he had done to me face. I refused to take my hands away from my face and he refused to leave me lying on the floor.

Finally I got up from the floor. I kept my hand on my face and pushed him away from me. I walked upstairs to the bedroom, closed the door and locked it behind me. I then looked in the mirror to see if I had any bruising done to my face. When I removed my hand from my face, I could see four of his fingerprints on my right cheek. No wonder he didn't want to leave the house. He knew there had to be damage to my face. This was the reason he wouldn't leave me. He must have known I was going to call someone, because this was the first time he had actually hit me with force.

I had enough. So I called my best friend to ask if I could come and live with her for a couple of weeks, until I could find a place of my own. I had been saving up for this day, because I knew I couldn't take the abuse too much longer. I asked my friend to promise me, she wouldn't call my sister and let her know what was going on. My friend said she couldn't tell my sister something that she didn't know. And then she asked me what was going on? But I refused to tell her while we were on the phone. I didn't want to take the chance of her calling the police on my boyfriend. I just wanted to get away from him as fast as I could.

I didn't want him to see me because I knew he would begin to cry so I wouldn't leave him. I was in no mood to listen to him begging and making false promises, saying he will never do it again. But I started to think. Nothing he did to me was done twice. It was always a different incident every time. So in a sense, he was right. Every incident was caused by a different reason. So again he was right. Every incident was caused by my actions which caused a reaction on his part.

After sitting on the bed thinking of all the actions and reaction and listing to him bang on the door to let him in. I called my friend and told her I wasn't coming over. I told her to forget about the whole thing and please don't call my sister. But she still wanted to know what happened. I told her that I would tell her all about it another time. My best friend wasn't happy with the decision I had just made, because I called her to ask if I could come and stay with her for a while. In order for me to call anyone and ask if I could come leave with them, something major had to happen to me. I tried to convince her that everything was okay and I had just over reacted to a situation that should have never happened. But she wasn't buying what I had to say. She said she just wanted to see for herself. She wouldn't leave me along. I knew if she was to come over at any given moment, my boyfriend would really be angry with me. Because he would know that I had to tell her something, for her to come over. It was so hard on me. I wanted her to come over because I needed someone other than my boyfriend to take care of me.

I felt like I was between a rock and a hard place. I thought I was going to lose my mind. I finally convinced my friend that I would come over to see her after I got off of work the next day. She accepted that offer and got off the phone.

I unlocked the bedroom door and let my boyfriend in so he could see the damage that was done to my face. After viewing my face and seeing his fingerprints, he really felt bad. He went to the bathroom and started a hot bubble bath for me. He then undressed me, lifted me up into his arms, kissed my face and laid me down into a nice hot tub of bubbles. While I lied in the tub, he went downstairs and poured me a glass of wine. He then picked out a book to read to me as I relaxed in the tub of bubbles, sipping my glass of wine. When he thought I had enough of the hot bubbled bath, he soaped a bath towel and began to bathe me. His touch was so comforting and soothing. I didn't want him to stop. I thought about him being on his knees and how his knees must be hurting after being on them for so long. I told him that I was ready to get out. He said he had one more surprise for me. He asked if I could stay in the tub just until he could prepare me for the next surprise. I was like a child at Christmas Eve night. I couldn't wait to see what I was about to get next. Finally it was time for my next surprise. He got a large beach towel to wrap around me, so I wouldn't drip water all over the floor. He wrapped me like a mother would wrap her newborn baby. Then he took me into the bedroom where there was a bed full of rose peddles of all colors, candles that lit up the bedroom and slow love making music playing.

As he laid me onto the bed, he had a zip lock sandwich bag full of ice to put on my face where his fingerprints were. First he kissed my face and then he put the bag of ice on it. He rolled me over gently onto my stomach, so he could massage me from the back of my neck to the bottom of my feet. The pampering went on for hours. The next morning he woke up early and cooked breakfast for the both of us. While I had breakfast in bed, he took his shower and got ready for work. I decided to see what my face looked like before I decided to get dress. The fingerprints were nearly gone. I had slightly red marks on my face. I was hoping that no one at work could tell the bruises that were on my face. So I went into the bathroom to ask my boyfriend, what he thought about the marks. And for some ungodly reason, this made him upset. I didn't know what the reason was. So I slammed the bathroom door and went back to the bedroom. He opened the bedroom door and asked if I had lost my mind. I told him yes. Yes I had lost my mind, because I was in a stupid, unjust relationship that I just couldn't seem to understand. One minute he was fine and the next minute, I never knew what would happen. I told him that we could have good days, good night and sometimes good years. But it never seems to amaze me how quickly those days, night and years could change in a snap of a finger. He raised back his hand to slap me again. But this time I saw it coming and moved to avoid the hit. I pushed him against the dresser. He hit his back on the corner of the dresser and fell to the floor. I grabbed my purse and ran out of the house. I didn't get a chance to finish dressing for work, so I went over to my friend's house. I got there just in time. She was backing out of her garage to go to my job. But when she saw me and the stage of fear, she knew something was dreadfully wrong. I asked if I could put my car into her garage, so my boyfriend wouldn't see it. She didn't ask me any questions. She just began to rearrange things in the garage so my car could fit into a space and not to be seen if she needed to leave. I didn't want to do any major changes, because my boyfriend notices any little change and I didn't want him to know where I was for the time being. After making all the necessary changes, my friend asked me, what was going on that was so bad, we had to rearrange her lifestyle? I began to tell her about how my boyfriend caught me and my boss coming back to the building after having lunch together. She gave me a crazy look. I told her that it was nothing. My boss and I were just friends. He wanted to take me to this new restaurant that had just opened, so he could catch me up with work. I had been away from work for six weeks.

My boss heard the food at this new place was great and he didn't want to go alone. My best friend said that it had to be more than that, because that wouldn't make me call her for a place to stay. So I continued to tell her the rest of the story.

I told her that I thought that her house would be the last place he would look. If he was to go looking for me, he would go to our friend's houses that we hung out with. She was the only friend I had that wasn't married, didn't have any children and lived alone. So I knew it would be the first place my boyfriend would look. We didn't have a home telephone and he didn't like for people to know what was going on in our household. So I didn't think he would come over and knock on her door to see if she heard from me.

He went to my job, sat in the parking lot and waited to see if I would show up for work. And when I didn't, he proceeded to call me. I had already called my job to take the week off. So when he called, the receptionist told him that I was on vacation. He knew the people I worked with knew I would always take vacations with him. So he asked the secretary, if she knew when I would be back to work. After sitting in the parking lot for days at a time, he decided to go by our friend's houses that were married or living the married life like we were doing. He never mentioned our quarrel or asked if they had seen me. He just acted as if he was stopping by to see how everything was going with them. Finally, he thought about my best friend's home. But he knew I wouldn't go there, because he disapproved of me having anything to do with single friends. He always said people that don't have anybody are the first ones to break up a relationship.

But that didn't stop him from waiting outside her home. He waited across the street, to see if I would leave or come over to her house. Little did he know. I was two steps ahead of him.

I never knew how long he had been on his job, how often he could leave or how long of a period of time he could stay away from his job. But I did know, making this move, opened my eyes to a lot of questions that I needed to know about my boyfriend. He knew everything about me and I only knew what he wanted me to know about him. After being at my friends home for four days and nights, I decided to go back home. I really missed being in my own house. Once you have your own place, it's hard to live with someone else.

I knew I was more than welcome at my friend's home, but I always had my guards up. I didn't want to do anything to cause trouble to her. I kept thinking about my boyfriend's jealous rages and I didn't want to get her involved. I saw my best friend changing her lifestyle to make me feel at home. It made me feel as if I had over stayed my welcoming. I felt as if she was ready to have her home back to the way it was before I arrived. Even though she never said anything, I could feel a difference. I understood why there was so much tension in her home. She was worried about me. I was living in her house, but I had her living my boyfriend's rules. I was afraid for her to have any of her friends over, she had to watch over her shoulders every time she had to leave her own home and she could see that something wasn't right with me. And I refused to talk to her about it. I didn't want her to have to worry about me. After all, the less she knew, the better it was for the both of us. She was truly a best friend, she never complained once about the way I had changed, but I could tell that she was feeling uncomfortable in her own home.

So one day while she was gone, I rearrange her garage back to the way it was. I left a note on her bedroom door to let her know, I really appreciated her being there for me in my time of need. I felt as if it was time for me to leave. I didn't want to ruin our friendship. I knew if I was to stay in her home any longer, it would have caused confusion between us. There were too many secrets going on in my life. It wasn't fair for me to come into her home rearranging things and making her life uncomfortable. If I couldn't be honest and talk to her about what was going on in my life.

Then why stay in her house and make her uncomfortable?

What I was going through was my problem not hers. So I wanted her to go back to living the way she was living before I got there.

When she came home and found the letter, she immediately called to see if I was alright. I told her I was fine. I was at the grocery store making groceries. She told me to be safe and she hung up the phone. By the way our conversation ended, I could tell she was upset with me. But I just couldn't continue making her life miserable, because she was trying to help me.

Just as I got ready to put my cell phone into my purse, someone grabbed my hand and took my cell phone from me. It was my boyfriend. He wanted to know who I was talking to and where had I been for the last four nights. I told him that I had been at a hotel. He wanted to know with whom and where was the receipt for the hotel stayed in. I told him I paid with cash and I discarded the receipt because I didn't want him to think I was with another man. I told him that I knew how he thought and it was always negative. If he would have seen a hotel bill in my possession, he would have accused me of having an affair, just for having the receipt. So I discarded the receipt. He told me that was the craziest thing he had ever heard. He said I had to come up with something much better than that excuse. I told him that it wasn't an excuse and I didn't have anything else to tell him. I said it was up to him to believe it or not, but I had nothing else to tell him.

We both were talking extremely loud in the store. We had caused a scene. People were standing all around us, as if we were getting ready to fight. The manager was called to the back of the store where we were standing. He asked me if everything was okay. When my boyfriend noticed all the people standing around us, he began to yell at them. He asked, if they had never heard anyone arguing with each other before. Then he told the people to mind their own business. He told them to go back to shopping, because that's what they came into the store for. The manager saw my boyfriend talking loud at the other customers in the store. So he asked my boyfriend what was the problem? My boyfriend answered, by telling him there was no problem, but there were a lot of nosey people in his store. Then the manager asked me again if I was okay. I told him I was fine and I was sorry for the commotion we started in his store. One of the customers in the store yelled out to my boyfriend, if he didn't want his business in the opening, then he should wait until he got home to pick a fight with his wife. My boyfriend wanted to know who had something to say and why couldn't they say it to his face? The manager asked us to leave his store. He thought it would be best if we came back another time when things calmed down. I took my boyfriend by the hand and escorted him out of the store. This did nothing but upset him more. When he got to his car, he said he was going to run me over for taking him out of the store. He said I made him look like a scary cat and he wasn't afraid of no one. I tried to tell him, that wasn't the reason I pulled out of the store. We had caused a huge commotion and the manager wanted us to leave. But he refused to understand. We were in separate cars. So I told him, I would meet him at the house.

When we finally made it to the house, I went inside first. The house was a mess. The rose peddles were still on the bed, the bathwater was still in the tub and the kitchen was a mess. When I asked him why didn't he clean the house? He responded by saying, because I wasn't there. He said I made his house a home and he just couldn't see himself without me. He said life wasn't worth living without me. Then he asked me not to ever leave him again. He looked like a sad puppy, with tears falling from his eyes. So I gave him a hug and promised never to leave him again. Then I told him to clean up the mess, because I wanted to take a long hot bubble bath to relax my mind.

Things were great for the next year. We were back to our old selves. So one day we decided to go to one of our married friend's parent's log cabin to do some fishing. The men were supposed to catch the fish and the women were going to clean and cook the fish. Well, my boyfriend caught the first fish and began to brag about it. So when the other guys started catching fish. Their total ended up being four each and my boyfriend had only caught two. This made my boyfriend upset. He no longer wanted to stay at the cabin. When he and the other guy got to the cabin, I could see a strange look on the other guy's faces. So I asked, what happened? This made my boyfriend angrier. He wanted to know why I had to ask if something was wrong. Then he wanted to know who died and put me in charge. Our friends had never seen this side of him. They wanted to know if I was okay and again by boyfriend had something to say about that. He wanted to know why everyone has to ask if his woman was okay. He wanted to know if I looked okay to them.

My boyfriend was so upset, he told the ladies to hurry and clean the fish, cook it so we can eat and go to bed. This offended our male friends. One of the men told my boyfriend that his attitude was uncalled for. He said no one did anything to make my boyfriend angry, so he needed to chill with all the smart remarks. My boyfriend then said we didn't need to eat their fish. He could buy fish that was already clean and cooked.

My friend's husband told my boyfriend that he had taken everything out of proportion. He said, it didn't mean anything about who caught the most fish. Everyone was going to eat as much fish as they wanted to eat, for as long as there was fish. Then he told me, he really didn't mean to hurt anyone's feelings. He just wanted to put everything behind him, cook the fish and enjoy the rest of the trip. My boyfriend got quiet. I didn't know if he had just realized, he had embarrassed himself or if he just didn't know what to say after our friend's last remarks.

Either way, I just wanted to hold him. So I went to him to give him a hug and he pushed me away. He said he didn't need any sympathy from me. He said he was a grown man and there weren't any situations he couldn't handle.

Why did I feel like he needed a hug?

The other couples looked at me as if they wanted to give me a hug. But they thought twice about coming towards me, since my boyfriend was acting so strange. Someone at the cabin said my boyfriend was acting as if he was on drugs. That thought never crossed my mind, but it could explain the mood swings.

My friend and I began to clean the fish. We seasoned and fried it. Why the men went into the cabin to clean themselves up. As we prepared the fish plates, my boyfriend complained about just having fish for dinner. He wanted to know, where was the rest of the meal?

When I told him that we were just having fish, he threw his plate to the floor. I immediately got up from my chair and began to clean up the fish.

My friend's husband said that enough was enough. Then he said if my boyfriend can't get it together. He would have to leave, because he was spoiling everyone else's fun. My boyfriend got up from the table and shouted, "Everyone else's fun. What fun?" So my friend's husband told my boyfriend, if he wasn't having fun then he needed to leave. I apologized to our friends, went to the back to pack our things and told my boyfriend lets go. Then he wanted to look pitiful. But no one gave him a second thought. He had just ruined their fun and there was no way they were going to feel sorry for him. My friend said she didn't see how I could put up with someone as miserable as my boyfriend was. Then she wanted to know if he acted that way often and if so. He needed help. She said he was like a time bomb waiting to explode and I should get him some help before something bad happens to me. Little did she know I had already been through a lot of changes with him. I took my boyfriend's hand, pulled him to the car and we headed home. I told my friends to keep the beer and wine that we brought to the party. Hoping we would have fun drinking it later that night. But because of the way my boyfriend was acting, I just wanted to go home.

When we finally got home, I tried taking off my boyfriend's shoes, so I could put him to bed. But, because I took off his shoes and not his pants caused him to go into a horrible rage. He got out of bed, grabbed one of his shoes and hit me across my head. I grabbed his other shoe, threw and hit him across his back. He gave me a look of surprise. He couldn't believe, I had just hit him with his own shoe. I told him that I wasn't a punching bag or something that he could take a swing at, every time he got upset about something. He had nothing to say to my remark. So I thought the conversation was over. I went downstairs to watch a movie that we bought to watch at the vacation house with our friends. Just as I was putting the movie into the DVD player my boyfriend made his way downstairs so he could watch the movie with me. I gave him a look of disappointment and I went back upstairs to take a shower. My boyfriend didn't like the fact of my walking away from him. He was trying to apologize, but I didn't give him a chance. So he followed me upstairs. He came into the bathroom where I was about to get into the shower. He grabbed me by the throat and pushed me to the wall. While holding me up against the wall, he began to unzip his pants. He was trying to pull out his private part to urinate on me, but this time I kicked him between his legs before he could finish unzipping his pants. He dropped to the floor and I ran to the bedroom to pick out some clothes.

I had made up my mind that I wasn't going to be treated like a dog. I wasn't sure where I was going, but I knew I had to get out of the house with him, before he did something to me that he would regret later. I wanted to go to the police department and file a report, but I was afraid of what might happen to him. There was something about the police that he just didn't like and I wanted to find out. So I went to the police station to file a report, but I just couldn't make myself get out of the car. I loved this man so much. I couldn't see myself being the cause of him being locked up behind bars.

After sitting in my car for about two hours, debating on whether or not I should go into the station and press charges on the man that I loved or if I should care myself home and deal with this problem like a woman in love should. I finally decided take myself back home, but when I got there, he wasn't home. So I took a shower and got ready for bed. When I woke up the next morning, my boyfriend wasn't home. He hadn't been home for the entire night and he didn't have any friends that would take him in for the night. So where could he have gone?

I was more worried about him not coming home, than I was about pressing charges on him. There was something special about this man that I just couldn't put my hands on. I knew he had a mental problem, but I didn't know how to deal with his problem without making him upset with me. Whenever I would ask him question about his temper, he would change the subject. So I respected his wishes and left him along. He was a good man, but because of his unusual temper, a lot of people didn't want to be around him. His temper even caused me to lose some of my friends. None of the people at the fish fry wanted to have anything to do with my boyfriend's unpredictable mood swings after seeing him in action.

They didn't understand why I would put up with someone who was rude and judgmental. He could find something wrong in every person he came in contact with. But when someone had something negative to say about him, he just couldn't handle it.

Just the thought of someone having a negative thought about him, would put him in an unhappy mindset and that's why I couldn't bring myself to ask him questions about his pass. I wanted to know, what happened to him in his pass that made him so astringent and mean. Because of my boyfriend's weird behavior, I just couldn't bring myself to leave him. I wanted to get help for him.

But how can you help someone that doesn't want to be helped?

I called a couple that was at the cabin with us the time my boyfriend acted out, and asked if they saw my boyfriend and they said yes. They had heard from him, but it was to apologized for the way he acted at the cabin. They said I sounded worried. So they asked if everything was okay. I told them both that my boyfriend and I had an argument and he left the house without letting me know if he would be coming back home. I told them that the argument was pretty appalling and we both said things that we really didn't mean to say. As I was talking to my friend on the phone, my boyfriend walked into the room and heard some of my conversation. He asked who I was telling our business to in a very nice manner. So I thought everything was over. I told my friend I would call her later, since he made it home. When I hung up the phone, he grabbed me by my hair and threw me to the floor. Then he got on top of me and slapped me very hard. He said that I was wrong for telling my friends, what goes on in our home. He said that I should treat our home like people treat Los Vegas. What's done in our home stays in our home. I told him that I was sorry and that it wouldn't happen again. But that wasn't enough for him. He said a mouth can say anything, especially when the mouth was mine. Then he told me that I talked too much. Everyone seems to know what's going on in our house and he didn't like that. So while he was sitting on me, he began to unzip his pants. I knew what was going to happen next, so I tried to push him off of me, by rolling over to the side. I thought if I was to roll over, he would fall off. But it didn't work. He rolled me back onto my back and there it was. The golden shower, but this time it was totally different from the others. This time, he looked me straight into my eyes while he urinated on me. The look on his face was devastating. I knew then, this strange behavior of urinating on me would never stop as long as I stayed in the relationship. I had to get out of this relationship before it was too late. While he was urinating on me, he made sure I couldn't move my arms to cover my face. This time he urinated all over my face. He kept repeating how I belonged to him and no one could take me from him. After he urinated, he sat on me for awhile. I wasn't able to wipe my face and it was the worst feeling ever. He asked if I knew how much he loved me. I answered by saying, "how could you love someone, when you use your urine to punish them?" I had never heard of such a thing. Why would a man urinate on a woman just to prove she belongs to them?

He said it was marking his territory. No other man wants a woman that has the smell of another man's urine. Then he tried to kiss me, but I turned my head. So he laid on me and fell asleep. I tried to roll him off of me so I could clean myself up, but he was too heavy. I couldn't move at all. I was so uncomfortable. I had no choice but to lay there with my eyes closed until I finally fell asleep. As the night passed, the urine got stronger and I could no longer stand the smell. So I began to call out his name to wake him. He finally woke up and I asked him to please get up, so I could take a shower. I had urine all over me, including my hair. He acted as if he didn't remember anything that happened the night before. I was so upset with him. I just wanted him to get up off me so I could take a shower. But he wouldn't get up unless I kissed him. So I tried kissing him on his forehead, but that wasn't enough. He wanted a genuine long passionate kiss, and he wouldn't take no for an answer. So at that point, I made up my mind to leave him. I gave him what he wanted. Then I asked very politely, for him to get off me, so I could take a shower. He asked if we could shower together. He said it would be fun. He said he'll wash my back and I could wash his. He had the look in his eyes that made me fall in love with him. It was a sweet, innocent, can't say no to him look and I gave in. We made love in the shower, but I was still leaving him. I was through with being urinated on. Most women would get urinated on while having sex with their mate and it was supposed to be a sexual thing. But in my case, it was a controlling issue. He would urinate on me, because he wants to claim me as his property. I was no one's property. We weren't married and I was ready to leave. I was sick and tired of being sick and tired.

My first thought was to go over to my sister's house, because she had an extra bedroom. But she loved my boyfriend so much. She wouldn't believe me if I was to tell her all the horrible things I was going through with him. I kept thinking about my boyfriend's final words to me.

He said that he would kill anyone that got in the way of us being together. With those words in my mind, I couldn't see myself bringing my sister into the picture. I didn't want to put her or her family in harm's way. I don't think that any of my family would believe how abusive my boyfriend was to me, because he was so charming whenever he was around other people.

My sister and I were so close. I knew if I told her what I was going through, she would be willing to help me. I couldn't think of anywhere else to go. So I drove over to my sister's house and sat in the car, in her parking lot. I had to get all my thoughts together before entering her house. She was a single parent because of her abusive husband. But her husband wasn't nothing like my boyfriend. So if anyone would believe me, it would be her. After gathering all my thoughts together, I decided to give it a try. I went up to her door and rang the doorbell. When she came to the door she had an unusual look on her face. She asked me if everything was alright. I told her that I needed a place to stay, because I had just left my boyfriend. She told me, he called her house looking for me earlier. I asked, what did she tell him?

She said she told him she hadn't heard from me. I asked if I could come in so we could talk. She told me that her doors were always open to me. I didn't know where to start because I held on to everything that was going on with me for so long. I told her that I was afraid of what he would do to her if he found out she let me stay with her. She said she didn't understand what I was talking about. So I told her that my boyfriend had been abusing me for a while and I wanted to leave him, but he refused to let me go. She asked why I couldn't leave.

I told her that he would slap me around and then urinate on me if I tried to leave him. She asked why I didn't call the police on him. I replied by telling her, I loved him and I didn't want to see him locked up. She became so upset with me. She said that my answer was the most brainless answer I could have thought of. She then told me that I was too smart to fall for something like that.

When a man puts his hands on a woman that means that he is a coward. She said that he knew I wouldn't call the police on him and that's why he did the things that he was doing to me. I told her that he said, he would kill anyone that tried to keep me away from him. So she said, let him try to kill her. She said she will be waiting for him to come over because the next time that he calls her house, she will most definitely tell him that I am at her house and he wasn't welcome to come and see me. I told my sister to be careful because he really has a mean streak in him. But my sister wasn't scared. She said he played that game with me because I let him get away with it. She wanted to call him up and let him know that I told her about his little silly game, he was playing on me.

When my sister looked at me and saw me shaking because I was afraid of what was about to happen, she called the police for me. But when the police arrived at her house, I froze and couldn't turn my boyfriend in. My sister was so upset with me. She said that she was willing to put her life on the line for me and I couldn't turn in a man that was urinating on me. The police told my sister that they couldn't do anything about the situation until I pressed charges on my boyfriend.

So until I was ready to turn him in, there was nothing that they could do for me. After the police left, my sister and I sat down and talked. I told her that it wasn't about my boyfriend, but it was about her. He told me that he would kill anyone that tried to keep us apart. By my sister letting me stay with her, I was afraid for her and her son. I began to think that I made a huge mistake by bringing my problems over to my sister's house. So I decided to leave and go back home to my boyfriend.

When I walked into the door, he was waiting downstairs watching television. He asked where I had been. I told him that I was out driving around trying to get my thoughts together. He wanted to know what thoughts that I had to get together. I said that I was unhappy in the relationship and I was trying to think of a way to tell him without either of us getting hurt. He had a habit of putting his hands on me, when things didn't go his way. Not to mention the urinating on me whenever he thought it was appropriate for him. I wanted him to know that I loved him, but I didn't like the way he was treating me. I felt as if I deserved to be treated in the manner that I treated him. I knew things weren't perfect with us, but who had a perfect relationship?

All I wanted was for him to stop with the abuse. Whenever he felt like punching something, he should go outside or punch a wall not me. He wanted to know where I got all of the suggestions that I happened to come up with. He didn't think I came up with these suggestions on my own. He asked again, where did I come up with the solutions for him to take his anger out on a wall or something outside? I told him that they were my suggestions and if he didn't want to abide by them, then we should separate.

Before I knew anything, he threw his cell phone at me and it hit me in the face. By the time I could grab my face he had jumped up from the couch and slapped me so hard, I fell to the floor. I saw his cell phone, so I reached to get it and he stomped my hand. Then he grabbed me by the hair and pulled me upstairs. He turned the shower on and held my head under the water. He said that no woman was going to give him rules to obey by as long as he was living. Then he told me to tell him who put those thoughts into my head, because he knew I couldn't come up with those ideas by myself. I refused to answer him. So he pulled me from under the water and kneed me in my ribs. He pushed my head back under the water. After holding me under the water for so long, he pulled me away again and asked the same question. When I gave him the same answer he would pull me from under the water and knee me in the ribs again. This routine went on for hours until he felt I just couldn't take the knees to my ribs any more.

I was tired from being held under water trying to hold my breath to keep from drowning, so he pushed me into the tub and began to urinate on me. He told me not to take a shower or a bath and I had to sleep in the tub until I could tell him who put those ideas into my head. I had my cell phone in my pocket, so I called my sister and asked if she could come over and pretend like she was coming to visit my boyfriend because he called her earlier and asked if she heard from me. Then I took a picture of myself lying in the tub with bruised ribs, from my boyfriend kneeing me over and over in the same spot, so she could see what I was talking about. My sister text me back and asked if I was ready to press charges. If not she was going to stay out of it. I returned her text saying I just wanted out of the relationship. I didn't want him to go to jail. I thought I heard my boyfriend coming up the stairs so I erased all the text messages, so he wouldn't know who I was texting or what I was texting.

I had to use the restroom but I was afraid to get out of the tub. I didn't know what he would do to me if I got out of the tub. He told me to stay in the tub before he left out to go downstairs. So I was trying to do what he told me to do, so he wouldn't hit me anymore that night. I waited for my sister to come to rescue me, but she never showed up. I guess I really made her upset with me, because I didn't want to press charges.

I guess she felt as if I loved my boyfriend more than I loved myself or her, because I told her he would hurt her if she tried to separate us, then I called her to come to get me. I guess I couldn't blame her for not coming over. She had a son to thing about and she didn't need to jeopardize her life trying to rescue someone that she knew they didn't want to be rescued.

What kind of fool was I?

Did that man really mean that much to me?

Why couldn't I press charges on him?

All these questions kept swimming around in my head as I lied in the bathtub full of urine. I felt less than a woman. I was afraid to get out of the tub to use the toilet. So while I was lying in the tub full of urine. I decided to urinate some more. I had my cell phone with me and even though I lied there urinating in the tub, I still couldn't force myself to call the police for help. I just wanted a clean sweep away from this man. But I couldn't see myself getting out of the crazy relationship in an orderly manner without getting either of us hurt in the process.

How can I say I love him, when he treats me like I'm not human?

Who does that to people and is it legal?

As I lied in the tub that night, I realized I had to find a way to save myself. I decided to take two weeks off work and seek help at a women's shelter. I didn't want my job to find out what I was doing, because I didn't want anyone to slip up and tell my boyfriend where I was going or what I was planning on doing.

The less everyone knew the better it was for them all. I didn't want to choose a shelter near my house or anywhere close. I was afraid he would find me and take his anger out on anyone he thought had something to do with me leaving him. I understood how my sister felt about coming to my house to try and rescue me. So I wasn't upset with her.

She had no rights to come into my house and take me away from someone that I refuse to press charges on. But if he was to come to her house to do bodily harm to me, she had all the rights to try and protect me. He would be trespassing on her property. That way I wouldn't have to press charges on him, because she could do it for me. But I would still be afraid of what he might do to her when he got released. So I thought the best thing for me to do was to contact a homeless shelter for battered women somewhere far away.

I finally got up the nerves to get out of my clothes that I was wearing and take myself a long hot bath. The mixture of my urine and his urine was very strong and had a foul order. It was the first time I had ever smelled something so foul. I wasn't sure if he had a urinary disease or some type of STD.

My boyfriend came in later and asked how long will it take for me to get out of the tub because he wanted to take a shower. I immediately got out of the tub, wrapped a towel around me and headed to the bedroom. He followed behind me. He snatched the towel off me and began to give me a body inspection. There were a couple of bruises on my face from when he threw his cell phone at me and slapped me to the floor. The bruises weren't too noticeable, so he thought nothing of them. It was my ribs that he was more concerned about. When he touched the bruises, I would clench in pain. He told me to get dress so we could go. I told him that I didn't want to go. He stared at me and said he wasn't going to tell me again to get dressed. Again I said no. I told him that I didn't want to be seen with him and I had no desire of following him around like I was his pet dog. He raised his hand back to slap me again and I just stood there waiting for the lick. There was no fear in my eyes. I stood there with my chest stuck out and my fist shut tight. As I was waiting for him to strike, he was waiting to see what I was going to do. I brushed up against him and went into the closet to find something to wear. He thought I had reconsidered and was getting dressed to follow him.

When he saw what I pulled out the closet. He snatched it from me and told me to find something else to wear. I asked why and he said I wasn't going with him wearing the clothes I had picked out. I told him I wasn't going with him and the clothes that I picked out were the clothes I was going to wear. I told him, if he was waiting for me to get dress and follow him, he would be waiting for a long time. I picked my clothes off the floor and went into the bathroom to get dress. When I came out, he was gone. I wanted to make sure he was really gone before I packed my suitcase and headed out to find a shelter. And not to my surprise, he walked through the door five minutes later. He grabbed me by my arm and pulled me down the stairs, out the door and pushed me into the car. He said when he tells me to get dress and to come with him. I am to do as he says and nothing else. I told him that I wasn't his child and both my parents were dead. So why did he think I had to listen to him. Even when my father was living, I didn't have to deal with the type of abuse that I was dealing with him. My father had respect for women and the way he was treating me was unacceptable. If my father had a glue of how I was letting him dog me around, he would be turning over in his grave. I was a very educated woman and I didn't need a man in my life to make something out of myself. I told him that I was a senior in college when I first met him and things were looking good for me. I had a full scholarship in engineering and I gave up my free education to be with him. I told him I was tired of the mistreatment and any man in his right mind would be glad to have a woman like me by his side.

When I said any man in their right mind would be pleased to have me. He slammed on the brakes, put the car in park and grabbed me by the throat. He squeezed as tight as his hands could hold around my neck. As he squeezed, he was asking me if there was another man. But I refused to answer him. So he squeezed harder. He said he knew I was acting strange for a reason, but if he was to catch me in another man's arms, we both would be dead on the spot.

He was doing exactly what I wanted him to do. Because I needed some kind of proof that he was abusing me. Now I had my evidence. As tight as he held my neck I knew he had to leave his hand prints on me, but I wanted more. I wanted to make sure I would get accepted into a battered shelter. So once he released my throat. I said to him, "I thought you said no other man wants a woman with the smell of a man's urine on her." As I said this to him, I was smiling at him and he couldn't stand it. He couldn't get to me like he wanted to because he was driving on the freeway. So he tried scaring me by picking up speed and driving reckless. I was so fed up with this man, nothing he did bothered me. The more he saw I wasn't afraid of him anymore the angrier he got. I began to put more pressure on him by teasing him. I was telling him to drive faster. Maybe he could kill us both. But he never took me up on my offer. He knew he was afraid to die. So I teased a little more and asked him what the matter was. Was he afraid of dying with me?

I told him to show me how big of a man he really was by driving the car off the freeway. I told him it didn't matter to me anymore, because I was already dead as long as I was with him. As I was talking to him, I was speaking in an annoying squeaky voice.

I was actually playing with my life, because I was dealing with a psycho that could snap in any moment and really kill us both at anytime. I had to put him through this test. Because he tested not only my heart, but my intelligence too, and the only way I could take back my sanity, was to get inside his head like he got inside of mine. I was a woman scorned and I needed to take back my life, even if it meant I had to die trying.

My sister giving up on me and not coming to my rescue really hit me hard. I wasn't sure if she was trying to give me tough love, to see if I could handle my own situation or she was upset with me for putting myself into this situation I was so deeply in. But either way, I had learned my lesson and I was ready for this lesson to come to pass. I swore never to let myself be misled again. Some people say you can't help for what the heart feels about another person. But a broken heart can sometimes be hard to fix and can sometimes keep you from finding your real true love. So don't rush to find the man of your dreams, because he might not exist.

We had been riding in the car for a while. He was quiet for the rest of the ride, which made me scared, but I didn't show my fears. I wanted to know where he was taking me so I asked him how much further were going. He had nothing to say. So I decided to enjoy the ride by turning up the radio. I wasn't sure why, but he pulled the car over, put in park and got out the car. He walked to the back of the car and leaned against the trunk. I sat in the car waiting to see if he would return. He started walking towards the traffic. I got out of the car and started calling out to him. But he ignored me and continued walking towards the traffic. I was afraid he would cause the oncoming traffic to have an accident, by trying not to hit him. I got back into the car on the driver's side, pulled onto the shoulder of the freeway and backed the car towards him. I asked him to get into the car so we could talk, but he continued to walk. Cars were going around him and dodging other cars. I yelled, "I love you please don't do this to me." He stopped walking, I asked him to get into the car, so we could go home and work things out. He walked over to the car and I opened the door for him to get in. I got into the passenger's seat and he drove us home. When we got home, he parked the car, walked over to my side of the car, opened my door, lifted me up into his arms and took me into the house and upstairs to our bedroom. We talked for two or three hours. He started off by tell me he was sorry for treating me like an animal. He said being in the military took a lot of effort. Some of the things they go through aren't allowed to be talked about. There were things he had to do that he knew wasn't right, but he had to do it or be punished. For so many years he held everything in and it hunted him from time to time. The only way to deal with the guilt was to latch out on the person that was the closes to him. He even wanted to seek help. But to do that, he would have to explain the reason for seeking help. He felt like he was in the position of being between a rock and a hard place. Many times he wanted to commit suicide, but he couldn't do it. There was no way he could take his own life. So he would put himself in a position for someone else to do it for him. He called himself a coward. He wanted to make me angry at him, so I would take his life for him. But I would never fight back. To him it was as if I had retrieved fire and that wasn't allow in the military unless you was order to do so, and I wasn't ordered to retrieve. He said, when he was doing all the horrible things to me, it wasn't me that he was trying to hurt. It was the enemy. So when I didn't fight back, I actually saved my own life. I heard a lot of horrible stories about the people who served in the military. But I was actually living with one of those people and it was scary. Whether it was the army, air force or the marines, I tip my hat off to them. Because I couldn't imagine the things they had to do, fighting to save our country.

After talking for hours, it was like a burden being lifted off my boyfriend's chest. I understood what he was going through and I sympathized with him having to hold something so horrible inside of him. He wanted to tell someone but he wasn't sure if he could trust anyone, because the secret was truly sacred. It's one of those secrets that you would say to a person, "If I tell you, I would have to kill you." He never told me his secrets and I really didn't think I wanted to know. Because I'm a sensitive person and I feel that some things are just meant to be kept as a secret. After hearing my boyfriend say he had no choice but to do the things he was told to do, and to forgive him for his bizarre mood swings and odd behavior. I couldn't help but to forgive him and give our relationship one last try. This was the first time he opened up to me. That night we became best friends again. I had learned something about him and it made me feel closer to him. He even apologized to our friends for his foolish acting.

I talked to my sister and my best girlfriend. I told them my boyfriend and I had worked things out and things were back to normal. My girlfriend wanted to know, what was normal and for how long I thought he would continue to be normal. My sister had nothing to say. I destroy the relationship between us when I accepted my boyfriend back. She didn't think for one minute my boyfriend had changed. She just wanted to wait and see how long he could play the game of being this changed man. Neither my sister nor my best friend had faith in me. They said I was the one that changed, not my boyfriend. I had no one to turn to if things were to go bad with our so called changed relationship. There was no one to interfere and that's what my boyfriend always wanted.

For the next year, he was the man I met in college. We moved out of our one bedroom town home and moved into a three bedroom house. We decided to lease the house with the option to buy. If we could manage to live in the house for three years with no problems, our next option would be to purchase it. Together we went looking for the extra furniture we needed to furnish the house. It felt good to pick out furniture together. I thought it was nice how we both had the same taste in luxury furniture. I always had an expensive taste, but I liked getting it on sale. It was nothing for me to wait until the price was right to purchase something I really wanted. We wanted to take our time furnishing the entire house, because we were undecided on keeping it. We didn't want to buy a lot of unnecessary things if we didn't have to. I've always wanted to own a house with two kids and a family dog. But my boyfriend wasn't too fun of animals. I think it had something to do with him being in the military. That was another subject he refused to talk about. After the first year of living in the house, I asked my boyfriend if he wanted to start a family to fill in the empty spaces. This triggered one of his bad reactions from the past. I knew he wasn't fun of animals, but not to have a family was something I wasn't willing to live without. For the first year, things were going great between us. We had little disagreements, but it was nothing to end our relationship.

I was tired of calling him my boyfriend. If I couldn't call him my husband, I at least wanted to call him my fiancé. So I asked him when he was going to buy me an engagement ring. I said, for as long as we had been together. I should be calling him my fiancé, not my boyfriend. So I thought we were ready to take the next step and start a family. We were living in a bigger place and we had more than enough room for kids to be added to our family. So I wanted to know, what the holdup was. I wasn't sure if the look on his face was a look of embarrassment, or a look of being upset at my question. Either way, I didn't get an answer. I started thinking about what my best friend had to say about my boyfriend not wanting to share me with anyone.

Could she mean that about us having kids too?

I never received an answer to my question. So that night when we were in bed, I asked him again about having a family. Out of nowhere, he turned over and slapped me in the mouth. The slap was so intense. It loosened both of my teeth. I wasn't about to go through the trauma we went through in the townhouse. So I reached over, grabbed the phone. I started dialing the police. I had made up my mind that this wasn't the man for me. Even though I made a promise not to ever leave him, I made a promise to myself not to be mistreated by any man. I no longer cared about his issues from the military. I only wanted to focus on my issues, being abused by a man from the military.

He knew I was calling the police. So he slapped the phone out of my hand before I could complete the number. He started crying and saying, if it was a baby I wanted then he would give me a baby. I told him I would be a fool to bring a baby into our relationship. I told him that I no longer wanted to be with him and I wanted to leave. He told me that it would be over my dead body, before he would let me leave him. I told him to consider me dead, because I refused to be treated in such a bad manner by anyone. He told me that I hadn't seen a bad manner yet. Then he grabbed a lamp that was sitting on the night stand by the bed and hit me across my head. The lamp broke in half and I was bleeding heavily. He wanted to stop the bleeding, but I wouldn't let him come near me. I didn't know how bad I was hurt, because of the adrenalin rush I had trying to fight back.

I fought back with all I had and when I wanted to give up. I fought some more. Seeing the blood drip down my face seemed to frighten him. But I didn't want to be fooled by one of his selfish tricks. He knew I would always give in when I saw him crying. I finally got close enough to the phone. So I picked it up and called the police as I waited for them to arrive. He knew it was over for us. He went into the closet and picked out some clothes and left the house before the police arrived. While he was gone, I packed enough things to live in a shelter for battled women. I had made up my mind to move on with whatever I could carry out that night. Everything else was materialistic and could be replaced within due time.

When the police arrived, they noticed my scars. They asked, what happened to me. I told them my boyfriend hit me with a lamp. They wanted to know if he was still in the house with me. I said he grabbed some clothes and left. They wanted to know if I knew where he went. I said no and I really didn't care. I asked the police if they would stay with me until I got my things out of the house before my boyfriend came back. They wanted to know if I wanted to press charges on him. At first I said yes. But the more I thought about it, the more I just wanted to get away from him and forget about everything that happened. The police asked if I needed a ride to the hospital because of my head injury. I told them that I could drive myself, but I would like for them to follow me. I just didn't want to be alone.

It didn't take long for me to gather more of my things. But I kept looking over my shoulder the whole time I packed. I was so scared, because I didn't know what would happen next. The police was with me, but I still had my doubts. After packing everything, I asked them if they could stay with me until I was released from the hospital. I just wanted to make sure my boyfriend wasn't following me. The police saw how nervous I was and asked me again if I wanted to press charges. I just couldn't bring myself to do that to my boyfriend. Even though he needed someone to stop him from treating women like they were animals.

I was sure. I wasn't the first woman he abused. Maybe that's why he never got married or had any children. I just hoped the women didn't stay in the relationship for as long as I did. I wasted a lot of years on him, hoping he would change.

When I got to the hospital, the police walked me in. I still didn't feel comfortable. I couldn't call my sister. Because she was still upset with me and I didn't want my best friend to know what had happened to me. The doctor had to put six staples in my head. I had to stay overnight just to make sure I didn't have any internal bleeding or concussion. The police couldn't spend the night with me. But they told me they would come back in the morning to check up on me. When I was released, I called my job to let them know I was leaving town and not to expect me to return to work for at least a year if at all. If it meant losing my job, I understood. I just didn't want to take any unnecessary precautions. I did some research on women shelters the last time my boyfriend and I got into a bad struggle. I found a shelter that I was really interested in. I didn't want anything close to my home or my job because I didn't want him to easily track me down. He was in the military and I didn't want to under estimate his skills.

The policemen that followed me to the hospital, kept their word. As I was getting ready to leave, they showed up at my bedroom door. I asked if they could follow me to the shelter that I chose to live in. I thought it would give me a better impression by having a police escort. When I arrived at the shelter, I had no problems being accepted. My face was bruised and swollen. I had staples in my head and I was a nervous wreck. The police introduced me to the director. She was an abusive wife and she came to the same shelter for help. It was a long time ago. But she devoted her time in helping other women that were in abusive relationships and had nowhere else to go.

The people working at the shelter were very friendly. No one asked me what happened to me. It didn't matter what I had just been through. They just wanted to make sure it wouldn't happen again. There were classes to attend to help the battered women get back on their feet and put the past behind them. They also had classes for women that were stay at home mom and didn't have any working skills. It was more like a self motivation class. It motivated women to go out and look for work with pride. I felt like I was one of the lucky ones, because most of the women had children living at the shelter with them. Not only did the mothers have to see a psychiatrist, but the kids had to see one too. I just hoped the kids weren't too dramatized, seeing their mother being abused by their father. It made me realize how lucky I was not to have any children. All of this was so different for me. I wanted to do something to help the unfortunate abused mother. So I asked the foundation if there was something I could do to be of some kind of help. I told them, I had money saved and I was willing to give to the organization if they needed it. They turned down my offer to give them money, but they said they could use my services in other ways. The shelter asked, if I would be willing to help with some of the classes they had for the more unfortunate battered moms. I agreed and I couldn't wait to get started.

There were women at the shelter that had no survival skills to make it on their own, with children. They were totally depended on their spouses. This was something I needed and I knew it would keep me from wanting to go back home to an abusive relationship.

When my parents were living, my father treated my mother like she was royalty. She was the mother of his children and he cherished her for just that reason alone. He was a strong man and there was no reason for him to prove or test his strength on my mother. That's why my sister was so upset with me. The drama I was going through was not allowed in our family. I had two brothers that were killed in a car crash and then there was my sister. She was second to the oldest and I was the baby. My father didn't let my brothers disrespect his daughters and he didn't allow them to disrespect their girlfriends. Neither of my brothers married. They were killed before having a wife or any children. My sister married at a young age. Her husband was abusive to her, but it was nothing like I was going through. My father told her that she wasn't raised to take abuse, mental or physical. He told her she was always welcome to come back home. But if she was to move back in with my parents, she had to divorce her abusive husband. My sister tried to stay with her husband because they had a son together. But my father told her that staying in an abusive relationship with children, only confuses the child. He said that the child knows what was going on in their home. So staying wasn't for the child's best interest. My sister took my father's advice and left her husband. But she didn't move in with my parents. My mother was fighting cancer and my sister didn't want to bring her young son into their home and add more drama to the family's home. She was more concern with my mother's illness.

Getting her own place was no problem for my sister. She was a college graduate and a working mother. She had a good paying job with great benefits. She secured a nice amount of money for hard times. So she wouldn't have to depend on living with someone. She wasted no time filing for a divorce. Her husband didn't give her a hard time about filing for the divorce. When her divorce was final, she went out and celebrated.

My mother died shortly after my sister's divorce. But she lasted long enough to let my sister know how proud she was of the choices she made. My father didn't last too much longer after my mother passed away. He died of a lonely heart. He and my mother were high school sweet hearts and he couldn't live his life without her. For months after my mother passed, my father sat in his favorite recliner, stared at nothing. He just gave up on living. He had lost both of his sons. There was no one left to carry on his last name to the next generation and he lost his one and only wife. He would always promise my mother, until death does them apart and he kept his promise.

I wanted to be like my parents. I wanted to be with one husband until death does us apart. I think my sister felt the same way. That's why she's a single parent. She can't seem to let go of her pass. We never had to think about calling someone else momma or daddy. Our parents were together forever. So finding another daddy for her son was something she never thought she would have to do. Her ex-husband moved on with his life. He has another woman and her two children living with him. My sister took it hard at first. Because her ex-husband spends more time with his girlfriend's kids, than he spends with his biological child. Her son was young when they divorced and he didn't understand his father having another family. But now he's much older and it doesn't seem to bother him at all. He's just happy to see his father whenever his father comes around. There were times when my sister wanted to move out of town to get away from her pass. But she felt guilty about taking her son away from his father. So she decided to stay and deal with the father son drama. It was much better to deal with the marriage drama, than to take her son away from his father.

I was recovering from my injuries very well. I had been in the shelter for nine months and I completed the classes needed for me to move on to the next level. I helped other mothers by coaching a class to help them feel out job applications and use good interviewing skills to get jobs.

Finally I felt safe enough to move into my own place. It had been nearly a year and my ex-boyfriend hadn't found me. So I thought he moved on to the next gullible woman. Little did I know? He was waiting for me to make my first mistake. So he could locate me. I was being careful not to back track anywhere he would be looking for me. I thought I had crossed all my T's and dotted all the I's. But I was wrong. Two months into my apartment. I got a knock on my door. When I looked out of the peep hole, I saw it was my ex-boyfriend. My heart hit the floor. I didn't know what to do. I didn't press charges on him. So there was nothing the police could do, except ask him to leave. I stood at the door in shock. I heard him say open the door. He said he knew I was looking at him through the peep hole. I couldn't bring myself to open the door. I didn't know if he would try to retaliate, because I left him, or if he just wanted to talk. Either way I was scared. He made it to be known. He would hurt anyone that tried to keep me away from him. I was the one who kept us apart. My heart was beating fifty miles a minute. I thought it was going to jump out of my shirt. After standing at the door for a while, he decided to leave. But I wasn't sure if he really left or if he was somewhere waiting to catch me alone.

For three days, I refused to leave my apartment. I had an on line home base receptionist job that the shelter helped me find through the program, because of my college degree. There were other incidents from women at the shelter, who thought they were safe from their abuser. And just when they let their guards down their abuser found them and finished the job he started. So the shelter came up with the brilliant idea of finding apartments base jobs to keep the women safe until they felt confident enough to go out. I didn't understand how this man found me. I was living in my apartment for two months, traveling back and forth to the grocery store and other places. And there were no signs of him being around me. My best friend, my sister or my previous job didn't know where to find me. I told no one of my whereabouts. I had been with this man for eight years and I had no idea what kind of job he had or what type of military skills he had to track me.

I had been with my ex-boyfriend long enough to know he was a great talker. He knew how to con something out of someone. A person would be giving out unwilling information without knowing what they had done. And when they finally realized what they had done, it would be too late. My ex-boyfriend would leave them with their mouth left wide open and looking dumfounded.

I was careful about letting anyone that meant anything to me. Know what was going on with my life.

After being cooped up in my apartment for two months, I decided I wasn't going to be a victim any longer. I had done nothing wrong and I wasn't going to live the rest of my life in hiding. So I opened my front door and walked out to my car. I didn't look all around me, because I didn't want to seem obvious. I didn't want him to think I was afraid of him. That would be giving him too much power over me and I wasn't comfortable with him having that much power. Whatever was going to happen was just going to happen. I was ready to take my life back. My first thought was to go to a place where there were lots of people. I needed as many witnesses as possible. When we were together, he didn't like making a scene in public. He had a certain personality, he wanted to keep, and I tried my best to help him maintain that image. Now it was my turn. I went to the nearest restaurant in the neighborhood, surrounded by plenty of people. I took my time ordering from the menu, just in case I had to leave in a hurry. While I was sitting alone I thought, maybe I was putting too much thought into this man wanting to hurt me.

What if he only wanted to talk?

So right then and there, I let my guards down. I ordered my food and when my food came to my table. I sat there and ate like a normal person without a care in the world. After I was finished eating, I paid for my food, got up from the table, walked to my car and slowly looked for the keys to unlock the door. Before I knew anything, he was standing in front of my car. I was no longer was afraid of him. He asked if we could go back into the restaurant and talk. I said there was nothing to talk about. He said his last words to me when he busted my head opened with a lamp, and I had to get six staples to close the incision. I told him, he didn't have to worry. Because I didn't press charges on him, I just wanted to be left alone. Like the night he left me alone bleeding to death in our home. I called him a coward, because only a coward would leave his woman at home alone bleeding. I asked if he had anything else he had to say to me, because I had already eaten and I wanted to go back to my place and called it a night.

He had the nervous to ask me why I was so bitter towards him. I told him, he must not have been listening to me, the whole time I was talking. Because I had my last straw with him, I lost everything that took me years to accomplish behind a man that only cared about himself. I told him that this was a new start for me and he wasn't in it. He said he wasn't through talking to me and there was something he had to get off his chest. I was done with trying to hear anything he had to say. He saw the look on my face. He said he really needed to talk to me. He said no woman hung in there with him the way I did. He then said he knew I loved him and when you love someone the way I loved him, it just don't go away that easily. He had a small box in his hand. So he opened the box and asked me if I would marry him. I told him no. It was too late for marriage. He had his chance to marry me and instead of getting a ring for my finger. I got six staples in the back of my head. If I was to agree on marrying him, that would mean I deserved any kind of mistreatment that came along with the package and I already knew what the package held. There was no way I was about to fall into that trap again.

He gave me the ring any way and said I deserved to have the ring, even if I decided not to marry him.

What kind of sympathy card was he playing now?

Did he really think I would fall for that line?

He needed to put that card back into the deck and pull out another one.

My life had changed within the eleven months we were apart. I saw things in a different manner with different terms. I guess one would say I grew up. I was on the same page with my father. When he said "if a man loves a woman, he would put her feelings first." And my relationship was nothing like that. My ex-boyfriend would put his needs first and he didn't have any room left to fit me in. My father had a lot of sayings, about how he wanted his daughters to be treated. My father was old school and taught my brothers to treat their women old school as well. They opened car doors, pulled out chairs and helped around the house like a real man should. My father called it, being a good provider for the family. He said when you respect a woman, you get respect back. My father wanted his daughters to think for ourselves. He said we had minds of our own and we were capable of making our own decisions. We should never sit back and wait for a man to tell us what to do or how to do it. He didn't want his daughters missing out on our dreams because of an overbearing man. He would say overbearing can become controlling and that becomes abuse. He was right all along. I just hate that it took me to live the life of a homeless battered person to see my father's point. I had lost everything I worked so hard for and I was ashamed of myself. Maybe the shelter was for the best. After all experience is the best teacher. If a person couldn't learn their lesson by an actual experience, then they would continue making the same mistake over and over again until they finally get it right. I just hate it took me eight years to finally realize I was going in a circle. Now that circle is a straight line and I refuse to see it curve.

It had been three weeks since my last visit from my ex-boyfriend and I was still holding on to the engagement ring that he gave me. I kept the ring in my glove compartment in my car. I wanted to make sure I gave him back his ring the next time I saw him. I tried not to go out much, because I was still feeling uncomfortable with our departure. I wasn't sure how he would react after I gave him, his ring back. So I kept a knife under my car seat. I was ready for whatever, was about to come my way. I felt it wouldn't be good, because he wasn't used to being turned down. My strategy was to go out and be around other people or to stay at home locked in my apartment with the phone close by my side. Either way I was going to be ready or die trying to get ready.

The unthinkable had finally come. I was leaving my apartment and he grabbed me by surprised from behind, while I was locking the door. Things weren't going in the way I had planned them to. Either I didn't think my plan out carefully or he was just two steps ahead of me. How could I forget about him being a military man? He was well trained for what he was about to do to me. He held his hand over my mouth very tight. I tried to open my mouth so I could bite his hand. But he was holding me too tight. He had some duck tape that was already torn. And in a quick second I had tape on my mouth. He taped my hands behind my back, picked me up and carried me to his car. He took me to another apartment complex not too far from where I was living. He was renting a downstairs apartment that was furnished with a twin size bed and a small sofa that's called a love seat. With a small flat screen television sitting on a night stand. As he took me out of the car and into his apartment. I tried to notice any and everything around me, just in case I had a chance to notify the police. My intentions were to come out of my situation alive. I had too much time to think about what I would do if I was to come in contact with him. For some odd reason I had a feeling, it would in up in the way that it did. I just under minded him. I wasn't prepared in the way I thought I was prepared. So I began to think wiser. If I under minded him, then maybe he under minded me. With that thought in mind, I started on my next plan.

The shelter knew about my on line job that I worked from my apartment. So maybe they would follow up on my status and well being. I wasn't sure how the program worked. But I was impressed on how they kept up with their battered women. In the four months of being on my own. The shelter called on the first of the month to report any changes with all their battered women. I never missed a call and I never missed out on my online job duties either. I hoped they would come by the apartment to check on me because I didn't answer my phone. My car was parked in front of my apartment. So someone had to notice something was wrong.

I had already started thinking about my next strategy. Just in case my first one didn't work out for me. I was willing to come out of this situation alive and if I had to use my ex-boyfriend to do it. Then that's what I was willing to do. All I could think of, was how my father would say never let a man under mind me. So I thought harder than I ever thought before. I wasn't going to be defeated this time. I was on top of my game and I was going to fight to win. I wasn't sure how I was going to come out, but my plan was to come out on top and alive. I was dealing with an old military seal warrior and he was good at hiding evidence. So that made it hard for me to think on his level. My first strategy was to get him to trust me. I knew if I could get him to trust me. He would eventually take the tape of my mouth and hands. Once I got him to release me. I would make him think that I still wanted to be with him. My strategy had to take time. I couldn't rush it, because he was too smart to fall for any of his tricks. I had to think on his level or at lease close to his level.

The first night was the hardest. I was too busy focusing on putting a plan together. I knew my plan had to be perfect or it wouldn't work. My ex-boyfriend had too much experience in this type of scheme. So I had to plan my escape carefully. I laid on the bed watching television as if I wasn't afraid. He eventually lied down behind me rubbing my hair. He told me that he was sorry for the way he took me from my apartment and brought me to his new place. But he couldn't risk me screaming. He said he never had any intentions of hurting me. He just wanted me to listen to what he had to say. I let a tear fall and when he wiped my face, that's when I knew I had him. He couldn't stand to seeing me cry. So I played it as my get out of jail card. I knew he would eventually release my mouth from the tape, because he kept on kissing me. After being taped for an entire day, he decided to release me, so I could eat. Later on that day he untapped my hands, he made me promise not to try to get away. He said he had a surprise for me. He took me by the hand and led me to the restroom. He bought me some beautiful lace sexy pajamas. He wanted me to take a bubble bath with him. So we could consummate the new beginning of our love for one another.

We sat in the tub for a couple of hours. He repeatedly ran hot water because the water kept getting cold. While I sat between his legs, he held me tight. He acted as if, he was afraid to let me go. The water had turned cold again and all the bubbles had disappeared. I was so ready to get out of the tub. But I needed him to trust me. So I didn't complain. I just sat there as he washed the same spot over and over. Finally he asked me if I was cold. I told him yes. But it was only because the water had turned cold. I thought he would add some more hot water, but he wanted to get out of the tub. He gave me a towel to dry myself off, while he dried himself. He reached for the pajamas he bought for me. He told me to put them on for him. I did as I was told to do. He picked me up, walked to the bed and laid me down very gently. As he walked around to the other side of the bed, he kept his eyes on me. He got into the bed and pulled the covers over the both of us. He didn't want to make love. He just wanted to spoon. So we held each other all night. The next morning we got dressed and he took me to a restaurant for breakfast. I thought he would take me through the drive through because of the type of situation we were in. But he took me inside. When the waitress came to our table to place the order, I tried to be as normal as I possibly could. He ordered for the both of us. We sat at the table as if we were newlyweds in love. Other people around us watched as he hand fed me. They thought it was cute. An older couple asked how long it had been since we were married. My ex-boyfriend said we had been married for ten years and the flame was still burning. The older couple thought his words were cute. They had been together for twenty five years and it was the first time for them to see a young couple married for as long as we were, and was still madly in love. They said young couples today don't know how to keep the kindle burning, but we seemed to have found out the secret. I wanted to tell them the truth, but I couldn't risk the chance of him trusting me.

We were back at his place, he told me that he was proud of me. He said he saw how I was fidgeting in my sit, like I wanted to tell the old couple I was being held as a hostage. I told him, he was looking too hard. I said I enjoyed our outing, especially the part of him treating me as if I was his newlywed wife. He began apologizing again, saying that it was his fault, the reason I left him. Then he started crying. He said he didn't want to lose me again and he promise he would change.

He said he would never put me through the things he did to me ever again. I no longer trusted him. So his words meant nothing to me. But I knew I had to continue playing his game. I refused to let my guards down. I wanted him to think everything was good with us. So I gave him a hug and that followed with a kiss. I laid him across the bed and began to undress him. But he said no. It was too soon for us to make love. He wanted us to get married first. I tried to tell him that marriage wasn't necessary. I loved him and he loved me, that was all we needed. He said he wanted our love to be better than it was the first time. Losing me made him realize how foolish he was and he had to make up for all he put me through. I told him that we were fine with the way we were and I was the one who was wrong. I said, I tried to rush him into marrying me, but now I see why he wanted to wait. There are still some things that we didn't know about each other. So the longer we wait, the longer our marriage would last. I told him that I wanted to know everything about him and I wanted him to know everything about me. This way we can't go wrong with each other, and our love would last forever. I noticed him getting upset with the things I was saying. So I kissed him on the lips and asked him what the matter was? He said he knew he messed up and he almost lost the best thing that ever happened to him. He promised if I was to give him another chance, he would be a better man. As tears dripped from his eyes, I just couldn't bring myself to say yes. I didn't trust him and he made the same promise more than once to me. My mind was made up. There were no more us. But how do I tell him?

Saying no to him is like playing a game of rushing roulette. I wasn't sure of how many bullets were left in the gun.

It was too late for us to try and fix what was broken. I had been away from him long enough to know he wasn't the man I wanted to be with. I had too much time to think while I was at the shelter. The programs and classes I took while I was there, thought me to put myself first, even though my father had given me the same lessons. I tried to maintain calm the whole time we were together. All I could think of was how I got away from him the first time. I had bruised ribs, a busted skull and a slight concussion. But I still got away alive.

If I was to make the wrong move or say the wrong thing to him, who knows what might happen to me?

I wasn't used to playing games, especially games that depended on my life. I began to think. Maybe I left the shelter too soon.

Was there something else I could have learned to help me get out of this situation?

How did he find me?

I was very careful of crossing my T's and dotting my I's.

So, what did I do wrong to lead him to me?

I lied across the bed and asked him if he wanted to join me. But he said no. He had other things on his mind. I said "I could really enjoy spooning with someone." And when I said the word someone, out came the ex-boyfriend that I was used to. He wanted to know who the someone was. I told him to look around the room.

Who else could I be talking about?

It was only the two of us in the room and no one knew where we were. He grabbed his head and sat on the bed. And again there was another apology. I was so tired of all the mood swings and apologizing. I had to think of something quick before I snapped and we both would be in body bags. I tried playing the sympathy card by crying. When he asked me why was I crying. I told him I wanted to go back to my apartment. I said, what he was doing to me was wrong and I didn't want to live like that. My sympathy card didn't work. Instead of feeling sorry for me he got very angry. He went back to his old self. He back slapped me and I fell of the bed. Then he came around the bed and picked me up off the floor by pulling my hair. I was crying and begging him to stop. But the more I spoke, the angrier he became. I thought he was going to kiss me, because I was still crying. But instead he bit me. His bite was so hard. When I tried to pull my face away from him, he bit down harder. My face was bleeding as I continued to pull away. Finally he loosens his grip and I was able to pull my face from his mouth. But not without leaving some broken skin in his mouth. He had bitten a whole in my face. I ran to the restroom to look in the mirror to see how much damage was done to my face. But when I tried to close the door, he stopped it with his foot. So I just let the door go and looked in the mirror. I asked him why he would do something like that to me. When all I ever did was loved him. He told me if he couldn't have me no other man would have me either. I told him I didn't want another man. I just wanted to be with him. But since part of my face was missing, I didn't want to be with anyone. I said that I didn't deserve to be with anyone.

How could someone look at me with a piece of my face missing?

I told him that I hated him and we would never get back together. He closed the restroom door. He pushed me into the tub and unzipped his pants. The next thing I knew, he was urinating on me. This time he only wanted to urinate on my face. I tried to cover my face with my hands but that wasn't enough. He urinated all over me. When the urine touched the part of my face that he bit off, I started to scream. It made my face burn as if I was put on fire. He then turned the shower on me. I wasn't sure if he was trying to burn me on purpose or the water was just too hot. So I jumped out of the tub. I grabbed a towel, wrapped it around me and ran out of the restroom. He sat on the toilet with his head in his hands, thinking about what he had just done to me.

While he sat there thinking, I opened the door and ran to the next door neighbor's apartment. I tried knocking on the door gently so my ex-boyfriend wouldn't know which apartment I ran to. An older lady opened the door. I told her I needed to call the police. She saw my face and asked if I was okay. I told her no. I said my ex-boyfriend jumped on me and bit off a piece of my face. I had on nothing but a towel wrapped around me, so the lady told me to come in and she gave me a house rob to put on. She asked if he raped me and I told her I wasn't sure, because I gave it up willingly to stay alive. I saw my ex-boyfriend walking outside of the apartments. I knew he was looking for me, but he wasn't sure if I would go into a stranger's apartment in the way that I was in. Normally I wouldn't go to a person's house naked and bleeding, but in this case I had no other choice.

I told the lady that I saw him walking around the apartments looking for me. She told me not to worry. She said, she had already called the police and they were on their way. Meanwhile, I tried to stay away from the window. I didn't want him to see me in the nice lady's apartment. I wasn't sure what he would do to her if he found me in her apartment. After looking around the apartments, my ex-boyfriend decided to get into his car and leave. But the lady took a picture of him getting into his car. When the police came, my ex-boyfriend was gone. Again they asked me if I wanted to press charges. This time I said yes. The lady showed the police the picture she took of my ex-boyfriend getting into his car and driving away. The police asked if they could hold on to her camera for evidence. They wanted to look at the picture that she took. The police took me down to the station. The nice lady asked me if I wanted her to come with me. I told her no. My ex-boyfriend had no idea what apartment I was in and I wanted to keep it that way. I told her that I didn't want her to lose her life, by trying to save mine. She told me she wasn't afraid of my ex-boyfriend and she knew what she was getting herself into. But I told her that I wouldn't be able to live with myself if something was to happen to her, just because she was trying to save me. I told her that I was with the police. So let them take over. She gave me her telephone number and told me to call her, if I needed anything, even a place to stay. I took the number, but I knew I wasn't going to call her. The less she knew about me the better it was for her.

Before leaving her apartment, I had the police to walk around to make sure my ex-boyfriend was gone. I didn't want him to see what apartment I was waiting in while he was looking for me. The police walked around and once they thought it was save for me to come out. Another police walked me to the car. The lady gave me a hug and told me I was truly brave. I told her that she was the brave one. She let a stranger into her home not knowing the consequences. I thanked her for being that brave person that had just saved my life.

Before taking me to the station, the policeman took me to the hospital. I thought I would have to get stitches in my face. But the doctor said the way my skin was bitten off, he couldn't stitch it back. He said it had to heal on its own. The doctor cleaned my wombs and gave me a technical shot because of the broken skin. I asked if it will leave a scar and the doctor said yes. He gave me some ointment and patches to put on my face and told me to keep it clean. I was released from the hospital and on my way to the police station. I had never been at a police station before. So I was kind of nervous. When we got there, there were other battered women and children. The policeman that drove me to the station took me to a private room and began to ask me questions about my situation. He wanted to know if this was the first time my ex-boyfriend abused me. I told him no. But it was the first time I wanted to press charges on him. I didn't know why, but I felt bad for my ex-boyfriend.

If he was to get locked up, what would happen to him?

Will the men in prison rape him?

Will he get beat up in prison, because he abuses women?

There were so many things going through my mind at once and I really felt sorry for him. The policeman told me if I didn't press charges on him, because of my injuries the state will press charges. Then he asked if my ex-boyfriend raped me. I said I wasn't sure, because I gave in so he wouldn't hurt me. They had to do a rape kit on me anyway. They had taken pictures of my face and it was reason enough to arrest my ex-boyfriend.

I asked if I was to press charges. Could they put me somewhere safe, so he couldn't find me?

The policeman said I was talking about hidden protective custody. He said they could work something out until my ex-boyfriend was found and brought to trial. The pictures that the lady took showed the license plates, make and model of the car. But when the police tried to find him, they found out that the car was a rental and my ex-boyfriend used a different name. I didn't understand how he could get a rental car without his drivers licensing, unless he had licensing in another name. I was beginning to think I didn't know my ex-boyfriend at all. I felt like such a fool. All the times I tried to save him from going to jail.

Now I knew why he would always run away before the police would arrive.

I was so upset with him I couldn't wait to press charges. He held me hostage in that apartment for three weeks and when the police went to check out the name of the lease. Another name came up. That name was different from the name I knew him as, and different from the name he gave for the rental car. This made the police suspicious.

They took me to a place that looked like I was in the country. I lived with an older lady and her granddaughter. I wasn't sure if they were in protective custody too. I was given a new name and identity to keep me safe. I wasn't afraid, I didn't even feel strange. I just did what I was told to do. The people around me made me feel right at home. I had always been a people person. So I just made myself feel right at home. I was allowed to go places, but I didn't feel comfortable leaving my comfort zone. I knew as long as I was in my comfort zone, no one would hurt me. I couldn't understand how someone could live their lives running from another person, until it happened to me. I started thinking about my sister, and if this was the reason she never dated after her divorce. I wondered if her ex-husband abused her to the point, she didn't want another man in her life or around her son.

The way I was living, was so beneath me. But I had no choice but to take what I could get. I didn't want to seem like I was too proud to be living where I was taken. So I acted as if I was part of the family. I hadn't heard anything from my sister or my best friend for a while. I was told not to contact anyone. Not even my own family members. I just knew my best friend had been trying to get in contact with me. She must be a nervous wreck. We hadn't talk for months, and she knows it not like me, not to call her or not to come visit her. My sister was so mad at me for not pressing charges on my ex-boyfriend earlier. I'm not sure if she misses me or not. But knowing my best friend, I know she went over to my sister's house to let her know I was missing. There was really no bad blood between me and my sister. We were just going through an unnecessary trial. Like most sisters do. I just hated we couldn't come to an agreement before I had to come to my new family to live. Maybe she and my best friend would put out a missing person about me. So they could find out I'm in hiding for my life.

Maybe that's just wishful thinking on my part. If it was that easy, my ex-boyfriend would have found me already. I never found out how he found me after I left the shelter and moved into my own apartment. I thought I did everything right to keep him off my trail, but maybe I made some kind of mistake. He found me too easy. So I must have made a mistake. I just hope he don't find me here. After being in hiding for four months, the police came to me and said they thought they had a lead on my ex-boyfriend. But when they followed up on their lead, they came across another person. This person was a criminal, but he wasn't the person they were looking for. The police asked me if my ex-boyfriend had any friends. I told them, not that I knew of. It was always me and him. He never brought anyone around me.

I thought to myself, maybe they found the right person and they thought it was the wrong person. My ex-boyfriend could have been a master of disguises. Or a man of many names and faces, I wouldn't be surprised if the person they caught and let go was really my ex-boyfriend. I started getting nervous. I was thinking that the person that they approached could have followed them to where I was in hiding. I began to worry myself sick. I could no longer eat or sleep. I was always looking over my shoulders and I thought I saw men that looked like my ex-boyfriend. I wanted to run away, but I had nowhere to run to. It was like being between a rock and a hard place. So I stayed locked up in my room all day. I didn't want to shower, because I couldn't hear if someone was to come into the bathroom with the shower water running. The bathroom was my scariest place in the house. When I would run the shower, the water would come out looking like urine. I was like a golden shower. I tried telling myself it was only my imagination. There was no such thing as golden showers. Maybe this was happening to me because the bathroom was the place most of my abuse happened. So I began to bathe once a week. I kept a knife in my bath water. Just in case I got too comfortable and let me guards down. Some people may say I'm too cautious, but I knew what kind of man I was dealing with.

Who knows how many women he put through the same things he put me through?

And if so, how many of those women are living?

How does he keep getting away?

Did he know someone on the police force to tell him my whereabouts?

Was he watching me all along and no one recognized him?

The more I thought about it, the more I thought the police had someone working on the inside for my ex-boyfriend. I was too careful for him to find out where I was. So the only explanation was to think that he had some helping him. I just didn't know who.

I was supposed to be under protected custody, but I didn't feel protected. I wanted to leave and find somewhere on my own. I thought if I could only go as far away as I could possible go, he would never find me. I wouldn't let anyone know where I would be. Not even the police. Maybe I was watching too many police shows on television. But I was pretty freaked out. My life felt like one of the characters on the police shows.

I wanted to call my sister and my best friend so bad, but I didn't know if their telephones were being bugged. So I laid in bed many of nights and cried myself to sleep. I couldn't eat, I wasn't getting enough sleep and I was a nervous wreck. I bit my fingernails down until they bled, without know the damage I was doing to myself. I had lost so much weight, worrying about my family and friend's safety. I wasn't sure if he would try and hurt my family, because he might have thought they had something to do with me being in hiding from him.

I was told I could stay in protective custody until my ex-boyfriend was brought to trial.

But what if he's never found?

Do I have to stay in protective custody for the rest of my life or do I go on with my life as usual?

How does a person go on with their life after being in such a horrific experience?

I couldn't just pack up and go back home, because my last home is where he found me. I couldn't go to my sister's place, because I wouldn't want to put her and her son in jeopardy.

So what does a person do in this type of situation?

I felt more afraid for my family and friends, than I felt for myself. I got myself into this crazy mess, so I felt it was up to me to get myself out.

So I decided to leave the protective custody place and find my own place. I was cooped up in that strange place for a year now and I couldn't see myself staying there any longer. I didn't have much to take with me, because all my things were at my last apartment. So one night while everyone was sleeping, I put my belongings into my car and left. My first stop was at my last apartment. I had to see if anyone else moved into it. I still had the old key, so I wanted to put the key to the test and see if it would open the door.

When I put the key into the key whole, someone grabbed my arm and pulled me into the apartment. I thought it was my ex-boyfriend, but it was a police officer staking out in my apartment to see if my ex-boyfriend would show up there. When they saw it was me, they were even more surprised. They wanted to know why I left the stake out. I told them that it had been a year and if they hadn't found him by then, they weren't going to find him. The officer told me that I was playing with my life by leaving protective custody. I told him that I made it to my apartment without anyone following me. I made sure I looked at every car that passed me and every car that was behind me. I even took different routes and ran a few red lights just to make sure I wasn't being followed. I told the officer, if I could just walk out of protective custody, how could I be protected. The office told me that I was a grown woman and no one had to hold my hand to stay protected. If I didn't want their help, then they aren't there to make me stay. What the officer had to say to me, made a lot of sense. But I just didn't feel save at the protective custody place. I felt like I was being watched constantly. The officer said I probably was watched. That's what protective custody does. They are constantly watching, so they can keep the people in custody safe.

I asked the officer if I could get some more of my personal belongings and I would go back to the stake out. He said there were no things. It had been a year and none of my stuff was in that apartment. I felt so ashamed. I let my thoughts bring me back to the one place I didn't need to be. The police said he would follow me back to the stake out, as we were leaving. He heard a sound. He told me to go into the bathroom. But I couldn't, because I was afraid of the bathroom. So I stood behind him. He thought he heard someone trying to come into the apartment. He whispered into my ear and asked me where did I park my car?

I told him I parked out front. Then he asked if my ex-boyfriend would recognize my car if he saw it outside. I said yes. I felt so stupid. After being so careful looking all around me to make sure I wasn't being followed. I parked my car right in front of my apartment. Now I knew how my ex-boyfriend found me the first time. He knew the make, model and year of my car. So it wasn't hard for him to track me at all.

My heart was beating so fast. I thought I was going to have a heart attack. So I ran behind the sofa to hide. When the officer thought I was safe and out of harm's way, he opened the door. But there was no one there. He told me that I was lucky that time, but I might not be as lucky the next time. I told him that it won't be a next time. Then I said that they needed to hurry and catch my ex-boyfriend before he finds out where I am. The officer asked me to have a little more patient with them, because they were trying to do the best thing for me. I told him that my ex-boyfriend was too smart to get caught. He was a military man and he had a lot of experience with hiding from people. The officer said my ex-boyfriend had a lot of experience with killing people too. So I should be more afraid of him than I think.

I really didn't think he would kill me. But I knew if he was to find me, he would urinate on me. I told the officer that he was doing a good job, staking out at my apartment. I said that I got to my apartment by myself and I can get back to the stake out by myself. But the officer wouldn't let me leave. Not until another officer came to follow me back to the protective place.

I decided to leave my car. Hoping it would catch my ex-boyfriend's eye. This way, he might think I was back at the apartments.

The police car arrived to take me back into protective service. It was an unmarked undercover police car and I felt safer. There was no way my ex-boyfriend would try and follow me with the police on my side. When I finally reached my destiny, I thought maybe this was the best place for me. I didn't know how many other people there were under police protective custody and maybe I didn't need to know. But it was a friendly little town and it was something I could get accustom to, if I really had to. The police returned later with another car for me. This time, I knew my ex-boyfriend wouldn't find me. I just hoped my strategy of leaving my other car at the apartments would work.

Three more months went by and still no word about my ex-boyfriend. So I decided to take a ride over to my best friend's house to see if she was worried about me. I decided not to call because I wasn't sure if her telephone was tapped. When I pulled up to her drive way. My ex-boyfriend jumped into my car and held me at gun point. He said he knew I would show up eventually. He said he had all the patients in the world for me. He said he knew I would come around thinking things were over and done, because no one had heard from him.

I should have listened to that officer at the apartment. He knew what he was talking about when he told me, I was lucky the first time I left protective custody.

I thought about my best friend. I wasn't sure if she was alright. The way my ex-boyfriend jumped into my car, there was no way my friend was unharmed. Then the thought of my sister popped into my head. She had a son and I was pretty sure my ex-boyfriend didn't care. I found him to be heartless and very short tempered towards people, including me.

When he asked me to drive off, I told him that I wanted to know if my family and friend were okay before I was to do anything. He said he told me that he would hurt anyone that came between us and he meant that. I told him that my family had no idea where I was or how I was doing. I told him that I believed him when he told me, he would hurt or kill anyone that tried to stop him from being with me. Again he asked me to drive off. But when he asked me the second time, he hit me in the mouth with the butte of the gun. I was so angry at him I just couldn't cry. I put the car into drive and I drove into my best friend's house. I began to call out her name but there was no answer.

My ex-boyfriend grabbed me by the hair and pulled me out of the car. He then dragged me to his car and tried to put me into the trunk. I refused to get in the trunk of his car. So he hit me in the head with his gun. The hit was so forceful. I was knocked out for maybe ten minutes. But that was just enough time for him to put me into the trunk of his car and drive off. When I regain conscious, I began to bang on the trunk of the car as loud as I could. I was also kicking and screaming to get anyone's attention. I had no idea if anyone knew I was missing. Since I left protective custody without letting anyone know where I was going or if I would be coming back. I had already left once, so I wasn't sure if anyone would look for me a second time. Then I got upset with the police department, because they should have had a police watching not only my best friend's house, but my sister's house as well.

My heart was racing and I was more scared than I had ever been in my life. I no longer knew this man that I was with and I didn't know what his intentions were. I did know this wasn't the work of a person's first time. I felt strongly in my heart that he had done this to another woman, if not women. There was no way a person could think of something, so vindictive in such short time.

Either a person had done something like this before, or they spent a lot of time thinking it through. And my thoughts were, he had done this to someone other than me. I thought about breaking the back break light, so a police would stop the car but it was too dark and I didn't know how to pull the plug out of the socket. I got the idea from a television show, but I wasn't sure how it really worked. I did know policemen would stop a car if the back lights were not properly working, just in case someone was in the trunk seeking help.

I didn't want to give up thinking of ideas to get away. I thought if I gave up then I would never be found. I was willing to fight all the way. My ex-boyfriend had finally met his match. This was one girlfriend he couldn't get rid of easily. If he knew I was thinking of ways to get away, for sure he would shoot me on the spot. So I tried to maintain my composure to make him think everything was okay between us. I couldn't be too obvious. Because he would know I was planning my get away. I had been in the trunk of the car for a while and I began to have panic attacks. I tried calling out to him, but he wasn't listening to me. He continued driving for at least another two hours. When we finally stopped, he opened the trunk and shouted I blew everything. Then he took me out of the trunk and into a cabin house that was decorated very well. He said I could have had it all, but I had to be miss goody two shoes. He said he had big plans for us and the cabin house was one of them. He told me that no one knew about the house and I was his forever. He said, when he meant till death did us apart, that's what he meant. No one was going to take me away from him, unless they wanted to die trying. I told him, what he was doing was wrong and he couldn't hold me as a hostage against my will.

He wanted to know why I wanted to get away from him. He said he tried so hard to make me happy and all I did was complained. He wanted to know what it would take to make me happy. I told him it would make me happy if he was to let me go. That would make me very happy. I said he wasn't the man I fell in love with and I didn't know who he was anymore.

He said he was the man I fell in love with. I just pushed all the wrong buttons to make him the way he was. I wanted to know what buttons I pushed. He was the one who changed. Urinating on me every chance he got. There were times when he made me keep the urine on me for hours at a time and that wasn't sanitary. That's when thing changed between us. I wanted him to treat me like a lady, not some stray dog. We could have had something special, but he became too controlling. In the beginning of our relationship, he wanted to be with other couples, but as the relationship grew stronger. He wanted to keep me all to himself.

He wanted to know where I got off talking to him in such a manner when he had a gun in his possession. I told him that his gun no longer frightened me. He had put me though worse, and I was at the end of my rope. I told him, if he was going to kill me than let's do it and get it over with. I was tired of talking and he wasn't saying anything I wanted to hear.

I had no idea where I was or how I was going to get away. But if he gave me just an ounce of leeway, I was going to run like my life depended on it.

As I was thinking of a way to get away, he pulled out a pair of handcuff that was attached to a short chain and cuffed me to the bathroom sink. He used the toilet as a table for me to have my food to eat and had a thick mat for the bath tub for me to sleep in the tub. He wouldn't let me brush my own teeth, because he thought I would use the toothbrush as a weapon against him. And he was probably right. If I could have gotten my hands on anything, I would have used it as a weapon. He wasn't the only one with skills. It's just that my skills weren't from the military. But they worked just as good in times of need.

I don't know why the police force couldn't find him. He looked the same. I thought maybe he had some drastic changes made to himself, so no one would figure out who he was. Maybe he was using a name of someone that never been in any trouble with the law. Maybe he was using another family member's name. After all, I had never met anyone in his family. During our entire relationship, there was no one in his family that ever came around. And since I only had my sister and she didn't come around either, I thought nothing of him not ever mentioning his family. I only knew his father was a military man and was very strict.

He made some serious plans to get me to that cabin. He already had clothes in the closet and he had the cabinets and the refrigerator full on food. He had everything set up so he wouldn't have to leave my side for nothing. Since I was cuffed in the bathroom, there was no reason for him to uncuff me to go elsewhere. He actually made it easy for me to maneuver around the bathroom without being uncomfortable. Everything was in reach so I couldn't complain. He had a small refrigerator in the bathroom with small water bottles in it. Just in case he had to leave me in the cabin alone, I would have cold water to drink.

He made me a nice comfortable bed in the tub for bedtime, the toilet tissue was on the floor next to the toilet for my convince and the handcuffs had a chain hooked to them so I had just enough room to move around to each place. But he didn't trust me with a tissue dispenser or a toothbrush. He was afraid I would try to use them as weapons. When he thought I needed to be cleaned, he would take the mat out of the tub, so I could bathe myself.

I felt my luck changing, because we were at the cabin for two weeks and my car was smashed into my friend's house. So I knew someone had to be looking for me. Because once the police was notified about my car being smashed into my best friend's house, they knew it had to be my car, because they were the ones that gave me the car. I didn't know if my friend and family were alive. I had no phone or television to watch, so there was no way to know if I was even on the missing person list.

My ex-boyfriend never told me what happened to my sister, her son and my friend. He said he wanted me to think about what I put him through. He said someone had to answer to my misbehaving. He said it with an evil smile on his face to make me think he punished my family because he couldn't get to me. But I wouldn't let him see the hurt I was feeling for my family. I was hoping the police had put my family in protective custody too. That was the only way I could stay focus on being away from them.

We were running low on toiletries, so I decided to make a smart comment, by telling him I didn't know what kind of women he brought to his cabin, but I like wiping and washing every time I use the restroom. He came into the bathroom and slammed my head against the bathtub. It didn't take long for me to know I wouldn't be making anymore comments or suggestions.

I had a knot on the back of my head as big as a lemon and a head ache to match it.

My ex-boyfriend was truly a soldier man. He kept a watch on everything around the cabin. He went without sleeping for days at a time, while making sure I wasn't trying to get away. When it was time for him to go out for more food, he would put a face towel in my mouth and tape it shut. He made sure I released my bladder before he took his long trips away from me. He told me I would be safe as long as I didn't try to do anything stupid. I asked, what was stupid? He made sure I couldn't call out for help and I was cuffed to the bathroom sink.

So how was I supposed to get away under my circumstances?

I was like a train dog. Why bite the hand that fed me?

I must say he kept me comfortable and clean under the poor circumstances I was living in. He hand fed me because he was afraid I would use the utensils against him. And he was right, at any given moment, I would have stabbed him with whatever I could get my hands on. I guess he didn't want me to go with him to get extra things needed for the cabin. I guess he knew I would try to alarm anyone that would listen to me.

So keeping me locked up in the cabin was his best idea for keeping me quiet. I was so ready to end the whole ordeal, being locked up and kept away from other humans. I thought I was going to go insane by the time someone found me.

I got, what was expected of me. The police told me not to leave protective custody again and I didn't listen. They said if I was to leave, there was a chance I might not make it back safe.

I should have listened to them. I didn't take them serious. I thought I had everything in control. But I was trying to live my life the way my father told me I should live it. I didn't want to be a handy capped person, waiting for someone to tell me when and where I could go. My father said I had a mind of my own and I should never be afraid to use it. Maybe this wasn't one of those times he was talking about. He also said God gave us common sense and I should use it also.

We had no television or radio for me to keep up with the news. So I had no idea what was going on with my ex-boyfriend's case or if anyone had me as a missing person.

I knew someone had to be missing me and what about my car?

Shouldn't someone be looking for the person that was driving it?

I felt like we were somewhere out in the country where nothing bad ever happens to people. So my ex-boyfriend had it made. No one would think of looking for an armed and dangerous man in the country where there's hardly any crimes, holding a young woman hostage.

That would be too much like right. So the chances of him being caught were little to none. As long as he kept me bounded and locked in a cabin's bathroom. He could have kept me for years and none of the country folks would have noticed. Because where ever we were, it was as quiet as a mouse. The whole time I was in the cabin, I heard nothing.

I felt so helpless with a towel taped inside of my mouth and my ex-boyfriend being gone for hours. If only I could have taken that tape off my mouth, I would have screamed as loud as I could for as long as I could. But I didn't know what good it would have done, because the cabin was off in the boondocks somewhere by itself. So screaming wouldn't have done me any good. I couldn't believe how well planned this man had everything. He was willing to drag our situation on for as long as he could.

Lucky for me, there was a person visiting where ever my ex-boyfriend was shopping. This person noticed a ring that my ex-boyfriend had on his baby finger. This ring that he wore was exactly like the ring this person's mother had reported stolen years earlier.

This person didn't want to accuse my ex-boyfriend of stealing the ring. Because he had a sister that was on crack and would sometimes steal from her family members. His sister was a runaway and she would often run away from home for days. But her last runaway episode lasted over a month and this was unusual for his sister. Her family filed a missing report after she went missing a year, but his sister was never found.

This person wanted to be cautious. Just in case my ex-boyfriend had something to do with his sister's disappearance. He knew my ex-boyfriend had something to do with his sister, because he was wearing their grandmother's ring. His mother gave a vague description of the last man that she saw her daughter with, and my ex-boyfriend seem to fit the description to him. So he followed my ex-boyfriend back to the cabin. He kept his distance, because he didn't want to be noticed. He felt he had a lead on his sister's disappearance and he didn't want to make any radical mistakes.

As he followed my ex-boyfriend, he remembered his licensed plate, color, make and model of the car. I couldn't believe my ex-boyfriend didn't notice someone trailing behind him. With all of the military experience he told me he'd been through.

How could he slip up and let someone follow him?

He was so sure of himself. He thought that he wouldn't get caught. He got careless and let his guards down. I guess he was so busy focusing on me. He forgot about the other women he put through this drama. I wonder if he knew they had family members that were looking for them.

The person that was following my ex-boyfriend, topped before as he saw my ex-boyfriend's car turn to come up the driveway. He knew where he could find my ex-boyfriend and he didn't want to do it alone. So he notified the police. I don't know what he told the police. But whatever it was, it was cause for the police to follow up and come to the cabin.

Because of that person's quick thinking, I was located cuffed to the sink in the bathroom. I wasn't sure who the person was or what the person had to do with me being rescued. But my heart went out to that person and I truly hope that person finds his sister. I never found out if that person was a man or a woman, because the police feared for their safety. And I understood why.

When the police entered the cabin, they didn't know what to expect. When they found me in the bathroom bound and chained to the sink, they released me and asked if I was in the cabin alone?

They wanted to know where my ex-boyfriend was, but I had no clue. I told them I had been cuffed to the bathroom sink for at least six weeks. My ex-boyfriend never let me know of his whereabouts.

The police searched the entire cabin, but my ex-boyfriend was nowhere to be found. I couldn't help but to wonder if he was somewhere watching the cabin as the police took me away. I couldn't believe I was found and they didn't capture him. I had to continue living my life looking over my shoulders. At least I knew he didn't know where I was kept in protective custody. He captured me when I went to visit my best friend. I later found out that my family and my best friend were okay. Neither of them was in danger. They weren't put in protective custody, but they were somewhere safe. They were told the less they knew, the better it would be for them. They were told I was in protective custody and my ex-boyfriend's was on the run. My sister had a large amount of money in a trust fund that she was saving for hard times. So I knew she and her son would be alright. My best friend had an illness that kept her from working and she was receiving a disability check that took good care of her. So it was nothing for her to pick up and take off. And that made me feel great. A burden was lifted off my shoulders, since my family and friend were okay.

I was the one who had to take a lost. I got my job when I first left college and I worked there for nearly ten years, before I had to leave, due to unnecessary drama. It was my dream career. I gave a hundred percent and was promoted at every chance I got. I couldn't believe how stupid I was behind a man that was so abusive to me. I guess it's true what people say about love being blind.

When the police got involved with my affairs, I was told that my ex-boyfriend was probably a serial killer. He dated two other women. That they knew for sure, but they weren't as lucky as I was. The police weren't sure if there were more women my ex-boyfriend had murdered. But they did assure me of two other women he dated before me were gone missing and they were still on the missing list.

I thought a serial killer was a person that kills multiple victims. But an officer told me that a serial killer is a person that kills in a certain order and it only take two to consider them as a serial killer.

It's as if he wants to be recognized for the type of killings. The way he kills is his signature and most of the time it's something about his victims that triggers him to kill.

The police wanted to know, what kept me alive?

Why was I so different from all the other women?

I told them that I didn't know of any other women, so I couldn't answer their questions. I found out that the person that noticed my ex-boyfriend was a grieving victim of my ex-boyfriend.

Nine years earlier, my ex-boyfriend dated this person's sister and she was never found. The girl dated my ex-boyfriend for a year and when she tried to leave my ex-boyfriend because of the abuse and urinating issue. He refused to let her go. But at least she confided in someone. She told her story to someone and that someone saved me. But she waited too late. My ex-boyfriend took her on a secret getaway. So they could work things out and the girl was never seen again. When I was told the girl dated my ex-boyfriend nine years earlier. I began to freak out. I had met him eleven years earlier. So that meant he dated the both of us at the same time. Another girl became missing two years later. She mentioned the urinating incident to some friends at work. And they told her to get out of the relationship, because the man had a serious issue. No one on the job heard from her after that. They just thought she quit.

All of a sudden, it hit me. I could have been killed by my ex-boyfriend a long time ago.

Why did he keep me alive?

I was with someone for ten years strong and never once did I think he would try and kill me. Maybe the person that noticed him when I was at the cabin had just saved my life. After all we were on a secret getaway trip that no one knew about.

I started to wonder, what was so different about me. We were in a relationship for six of those ten years that he was with the other girl. What I didn't understand, was the fact of him keeping his same name and was never caught. Most people that are on the run would change their names but use the same initials, or change their appearance, so they couldn't be recognized. But not my ex-boyfriend, he kept his same name and his same identity.

I was later told, he kept the same name, but the name wasn't his name. He was using the name of his dead father who was a military man. But his father was a senior and he was a junior. So all the stories my ex-boyfriend was telling me were stories of his father.

Because of my ex-boyfriend's history, I was never told who found me at the cabin. But I was thankful for what was done in my favor. I felt bad for the other two women and I know someday my ex-boyfriend would have his day in court. One day he's going to slip up, like he slipped up at the cabin that led the police to find me. I couldn't believe I didn't want to press charges on him in the beginning of our relationship. But maybe not pressing charges is what saved my life. It wasn't until I pressed charges and was put under protective custody, made him bring me to the secret getaway.

How many women did he bring to the getaway cabin?

I didn't like mentioning the urinating situation because it was embarrassing and degrading. I knew it had to be the information that the police needed to catch him. So I put my pride behind me and did what I had to do to try and stop my ex-boyfriend before he hurt any other women. There were other women missing from the town that my ex-boyfriend's previous victim came from. But no one ever mentioned the part about the girls being urinated on. Once the police mentioned they were looking for a man that may be a serial killer that urinates on his victims. Other people will recognized his tactics and call the police with other leads. I really felt like we were on to something, once I mentioned the urinating process. No one had ever mentioned it and now it seemed to be my ex-boyfriend's calling card. If he was truly a serial killer, he had to treat every woman he dated the same way.

I told the police, there were times when my ex-boyfriend would abuse me and would leave the house for hours. And when he came back, he would be very emotional and apologetic. But there was never any reason for me to think he had done something wrong or hurtful to someone else. So I would just hold him tight and forgive him for the actions he made towards me.

I couldn't help but wonder if my ex-boyfriend was out killing other women to save me. He always said I was the chosen one and that he would never trade me in for nothing. He had never been with a woman for as long as he had been with me. So maybe his strategy was to harm other women in the place of me, because he loved me too much to kill me. I was actually just saying something to help the policemen out. I really didn't want to think my life was saved, in place of another person's life. That would be something that would stay on my heart for as long as I lived. Knowing someone else took my place in death and all because I was too ashamed of mentioning him urinating on me.

The police checked the cabin for evidences of other victims, but they didn't find anything. They even brought out dogs to sniff for dead buried bodies and again nothing was found. So either my ex-boyfriend was good at what he was doing or he wasn't guilty of the crimes he was being charged with. He couldn't be that gullible to stay somewhere and become recognized by other people.

How does a person get rid of a dead body without leaving any evidence?

Could this be the reason he urinated on his victims?

Was he using his urine to hide the scent of his victims from the dogs?

I began to wonder if he really was a military man after all. Or was that something he used to justify his weird doglike behavior?

I wasted a lot of years with this man, trying to make excuses for his twisted mood swings and physical abuse. I guess my father was right when he said "A man would let you know, what he wants you to know and if he didn't want you to know, then you would never find out." And with those words, he would tell me and my sister to do our own research. Never let a man lead you on without knowing the truth about him.

But this man was so sweet and innocent in the beginning of our relationship. I just didn't think I had to research him. He had a typical excuse for his massive mood swings and I believed every word. His lies were so real and convincing. I couldn't help but to fall in love with him over and over again.

We both came into the relationship without any children and we seemed to be so compatible at the time. It seemed as if we both wanted and desired the same things out of life. He was highly educated and so was I. So we moved into our first place together not knowing enough about one another, but it felt right. I knew he had a short temper, but that was something I could live with. Until two years into our relationship, he began urinating on me.

Who does that to people?

He had to have a reason for his urine issue, other than marking his territory. I just couldn't figure it out. Until the police said they couldn't find any of his victims. I tried to think of him eating or drinking anything to make his urine stronger to throw the dogs off his tracks. But there was nothing I could think of. The dogs had to have a scent of my ex-boyfriend, because he was in the cabin with me for six weeks. I knew his scent had to be somewhere in the bathroom because my ex-boyfriend urinated on me while I was lying in the tub on the mat.

I was no detective, but I knew the dogs had to find something other than my sent in the cabin. I watched as the dogs sniffed around the cabin and found nothing. But to me, it just wasn't enough. I wanted to see some kind of proof of the allegations that were being brought upon my ex-boyfriend. It was hard for me to except the term, serial killer. Yes, there were people missing, but without any evidence, to go alone with the things my ex-boyfriend was being accused of doing. Made it even harder for me to believe he killed people. I wanted some kind of proof of the alleged killings, because without any proof, my ex-boyfriend was still considered innocent.

There was only one person at the scene claiming to be a victim's brother, but the person didn't want to be identified. Because of this person, I was found and I am forever grateful for what this person done by bringing the police to my aide.

I had been through a lot with my ex-boyfriend and I was willing to do whatever it took to make our relationship work. I didn't have much experience in long lasting relationships, because I wanted to get an education first. I also had a zero tolerance policy that I was working on. I was told that a man would do whatever they were allowed to do. So I decided to set my bar high. The guys I dated before my ex-boyfriend didn't last long because of the rules I had. So when I met my ex-boyfriend, I decided to change my rules. He seemed to be very intelligent, handsome and polite person. And I figured it was time for me to settle down.

When I think about the years, I spent with a man I barely knew. My life was in jeopardy when he first laid eyes on me. I was to be his next victim. But for some odd reason, he fell in love with me. I was told by the police. That his last victim's family member said he refused to let his women be opinionated. But I came into the relationship already open minded, opinionated and strong willed. He knew I was a college student, working on my degree and I had lots of opinions. I think that's what interested him the most about me. I was a strong willed person who knew what I wanted. But later into the relationship, things began to change. He became more demanding and controlling with almost everything we did together.

I could only hope that I gave the police enough information about my ex-boyfriend to help them find him. I didn't want another woman to have to go through what I or any of the other women went through, by dating this man. My ex-boyfriend could be a real charmer in the beginning, but like everything else in life, it changes.

When I finally left the cabin, I felt my ex-boyfriend's eyes watching me. He had to be somewhere close by, because he never made it home from wherever he when.

I was taken to the hospital first for x-rays because of the knot the size of a lemon on the back of my head from when I was slammed against the tub in the bathroom. They also wanted to do another rape kit. When I was released from the hospital, there were two police cars waiting to take me to protective services again. After being in protective custody for two additional years, I gained thirty pounds which looked good on me. I had finally given up on the police ever catching my ex-boyfriend. So I decided to take a new identity. I cut and color my hair and I moved to California to start my life over. I kept my first name but changed my middle and last name, so it wouldn't be so obvious to anyone. Shortly after moving to California, I got a job offer from a person I went to college with. When he asked me about my life after college, I told him I got married, got divorced and kept my married name. But no one really knew my middle name, so there was no need for any explanation for changing it.

My sister blamed me for having to change her life. She had to move from her comfortable home, to somewhere far away from her ex-husband. Because of my life's drama, so we never spoke to one another again. My best friend found herself a good man and got married and was working on her second child. So I left her alone to deal with her married life. I hadn't heard from her since. So I decided to do me. I got a job working with children with special needs, at a company that paid pretty good money. I had weekends off and I spent a lot of my time at the California beaches. I was pretty dramatized with my last relationship. So I used my time wisely with the kids at my job.

Starting over seemed to come natural for me, I enjoyed the weather in California. I made enough money to support myself. I lived alone. I had no one to answer to but myself, and it felt good. I wanted to take my time with decorating my place, because I wasn't too sure on how long I would be staying there. I liked where I was, but I wanted to be closer to my job. Sometimes I would work double shifts to occupy my time. I was skeptical about meeting men, because of my last relation and in California lots of men were in gangs. So I tried to keep up with the color code of all gangs. Everything I needed and wanted was in California. I could work as many hours as I wanted, I could make as much money as I wanted and the beaches were there.

My weakness was clothes. I always loved clothes. I had to get rid of all my old clothes because of the weight I put on. But I must say my weight looked good on me. I went from a size three to a size six. I had no stomach, a nice butte and my legs were gorgeous. I must admit I was blessed with my mother's big beautiful legs. Something that drove my father crazy, I didn't think I would look good with short hair, but it's so easy to maintain and I didn't have to worry about anyone pulling my long hair and dragging me across the floor anymore. I think I'll keep it short. I never got the chance to have any children and I always hated my ex-boyfriend for that. He took the only child I probably would have, by pushing me down those stairs. I can't help but think about my baby, when I'm working with other children. I guess that's why I love my job so much. Working the extra hours doesn't seem to bother me at all. I know I'm supposed to leave my past behind me, but I can't help but wonder if my ex-boyfriend was ever caught. When I'm at work with the other women and they are all talking about their families, I just sit and listen. When they ask me about my family, I lie and tell them that I was an only child and both parents were killed in a car accident. I've even told them about my miscarriage and how I lost my baby. But my ex-boyfriend is never mentioned.